The Last Slide

A PHOEBE KORNEAL MYSTERY SERIES

BOOK 2

The Last Slide

A Phoebe Korneal Mystery

GaGa Gabardi & Judilee Butler

The Last Slide

PHOEBE KORNEAL MYSTERY SERIES

BOOK 2

FIRST EDITION

Soft Cover:
13 ISBN: 978-1-7361239-1-1

This story is dedicated to our husbands

David & Duane

We so love your support, encouragement,
and the occasional unsolicited critiques.

CONTENTS

YOU ARE HERE

↓

INTRODUCTION

O ur fictional setting is the town of Oresville, Green County, Colorado, and a recent census puts the population near 2,000, including every known dog, cat, and various critters. The citizens of Oresville thrive in today's setting at over 10,000 feet in altitude with a foothold in the mining spirit of the mid-1800s. Although several of our characters have relocated to Oresville from other states, they feel the acceptance and camaraderie of those who were born and raised in this high mountain town.

Phoebe Korneal, Green County Deputy Sheriff and *detective as needed* is one of those transplants. She has enjoyed becoming part of this close-knit community. Several months have passed since she solved the mystery of the death of Old Al and now in this holiday season yet another mystery has developed in Oresville. A truck was found off a mountain road, partially covered in snow. It appears there may be a person inside . . . dead or worse! How did this happen? Was this an accident caused by poor judgement or was there something more sinister afoot? Who is in the truck and whose truck is it? Phoebe has her work cut out for her as she does her best to enjoy Christmas and the anticipation of a special New Year's Eve.

In a small town such as Oresville anything that happens to visitors or residents draws attention and concern, creating a headline. Phoebe's childhood friend, Carrie Jean, Ace Reporter for the High Mountain Gazette and the daily digital newsletter, the e-Blast! stands ready to inform the public. Something as mild as a weather report can be a vital piece of information for this hamlet at nearly 10,500 feet above sea level. CJ reports everything in the traditional role of newspapers in settling the western territories and bringing "community" to those roughshod settlements. Today these early startups are the thriving towns and cities of Colorado and newspapers remain integral players just as when the state was getting its footing settling the West in the 1800s.

We thank the National Hall of Fame and Mining Museum in Leadville, Colorado for the historical value it preserves for this state and its many visitors. Mountain settlements in the 1800s were not for the faint of heart and this museum does a great job at documenting the history and challenges of life in the 1800s, as well as recognizing and honoring the many strong-minded and adventurous people attracted to mining. The history of the area supports the continuing independent culture of the state. Anyone interested in Colorado history must start the study with a trip to this mining museum.

Still today mining is part and parcel to the free-spirited, self-reliant people who seek their fortune in gold in the high mountains of the Centennial State. The Rocky Mountains draw those who value the great out-of-doors and a culture of collective yet independent residents who appreciate and strive to preserve the environment. This is the perspective we bring to Oresville and our characters.

Join Phoebe and her crew of interesting and somewhat eccentric fellow Oresvillians to unravel the mystery of this truck off the high mountain trail. As the end of the year approaches and the seasonal celebrations unfold in Oresville, the depth of winter is upon our characters. This light murder mystery will keep you warm at night and bring a smile as you escape to the high mountains of Colorado. Read on!

SLIDE ON OVER

The phone rang too loudly in the stillness of the Sheriff's front office. Nothing much happened during the end-of-year holidays. The quiet was a welcome relief from the usual level of activity with phones ringing non-stop, people laughing over shared obscure events, machines spitting out paper, and citizens waiting for help. Law enforcement seemed to take a quiet step back with fewer people working their shifts because of vacations or vacation-mindedness. Perhaps it was a collective deep breath before the anticipated New Year's Eve disturbances and overindulgences.

The sudden ringing took Roz's attention from her latest manicure to the business at hand. She fumbled the headset into place, grabbed a pen with an announcement, "Good morning. Green County Sheriff's Office. Rosalind Marie Beaudreau speaking."

"Roz, for God's sake, it's me, Augusta." She was speaking as though in a big hurry while trying to talk over the heavy machine noise in the background.

"This doesn't bode well, Augusta. You only call this number when there's a problem."

"Well, you got that right. Queennie and I are runnin' our machines below Slide Lake along the Wurtz Ditch Road."

Roz did an eye roll, as she swished her long black hair to the back and tied it back over itself into a messy bun. She tapped her pen thinking, *OK. OK. Get on with it. Nice that you're runnin' or something by a ditch with a machine and I'm working. This whole thing sounds weird, maybe even kinky?*

Putting down the pen, she smiled to herself as she lounged back into the ancient wooden office chair. Roz held up both hands to recheck today's polish job, applied before anyone had come into the office, of course. If the bottom drawer of her desk at the Sheriff's office were opened, a miniature drugstore cosmetic counter could be found. Roz liked to be ready for any last-minute touch-up should a good-looking, single, male citizen step into the Green County Sheriff's offices in need of help.

Comfortable enough for listening, Roz teased in the thickest Cajun English accent she could muster, "So y'all are runnin' a machine and called to chit-chat with me about it? I'm workin' here, ya know." Originally from the Cajun Country of Louisiana, she could pour on the Louisiana twang as the situation dictated.

"Yah, yah. I know, but that's not why I'm callin'. With the great snow up here yesterday, we're trying out our snowmobiles with a few other buddies. Just a friendly little ride up the Forest Service trail to enjoy the result of yesterday's storm. It's been nothing but a dirt trail this winter with the drought and all. Did I tell ya Queennie got a machine?"

Losing interest in the nail polish and this conversation, Roz mumbled, "No, hadn't heard that, but back to why y'all are callin' on an official recorded line?"

Sometimes Augusta needed a little nudge to get back on point. She lived all summer at her silver mine, The Last Hurrah, mostly by herself with the limited company of the summer hire kids. She employed several mining engineering students each summer in an effort to support the mining industry going forward. Old enough to be their grandmother, or their great-grandmother in some cases, their social scales were quite different. In the winter, she moved back to town to run her businesses, socialize, and participate in the action of Oresville. It was similar to catching up to the town's events after a quiet summer in the mountains. Her businesses took little of her time and seldom was any direct control needed. Ss the third-generation owner, Augusta has set up processes that virtually guaranteed good hired help, an easy-going attitude, and solid pay with benefits. This kept everything moving smoothly while she enjoyed the great Colorado outdoors during each of the four seasons.

"Oh, yea, right." She paused and Roz could almost taste a change over the airwaves. Augusta dropped the chatty talk and added in a tense, quick voice, "Well, we came across a small, red pickup off the road. It's situated on the side of a gully, almost covered in snow, hung up on some thick pine trees. It could be No-Name Gulch, but hard to tell with what the storm brought in yesterday. The wind blew away some of the snow from the leeward side and it looks like someone's in it, not moving. Maybe unconscious—maybe dead or worse. Can't be sure from up here on the road. Better get Sheriff Joe up here pronto."

Snapping to attention, Roz sat up straight and slid to the edge of her chair, pressing the ear pieces tight to her ears to be sure she had heard correctly. She was looking around the empty public entrance area of the Sheriff's Office, searching for anyone who could help while thinking about the next steps all at the same time. "You got it, Augusta."

Roz's training clicked in. "Wait. I'm thinkin' we need search and rescue for this one. Can ya give me your exact location?"

Augusta dropped back to her conversational rambling again, "Oh, you know it's up the trail towards Slide Lake, above the Azure Lakes. The sun is exploding off all this fresh snow, practically blinding us. We followed Wurtz's Ditch if ya know where that is.

"The coordinates, *please*, Augusta, Wurtz Whatever is nada to me. Remember I'm a Cajun Gal, not a Mountain Momma." Roz tried to keep the impatience out of her voice, but could feel the tension grow as she tried to coax Augusta for the information needed.

"Oh, sure. Right. Here's the GPS coordinates."

Roz was typing the numbers into the Green County's Emergency System, repeating back each of the numerals with her voice rising enough to be heard by anyone within a thousand yards, all while nodding in agreement with herself, "Great. I'll see that Joe and the rescue team get right on this. Hang tight, Sista'. Help'll be there soon." With her anxiety now running rampant, she let go with a yell, "And don't y'all do anything crazy like trying to implement your own rescue. If a person is in there, leave it for the experts." Roz stopped, took a breath to get back to a reassuring level, and lowered her voice to a scolding. "Don't touch anything! Ya hear me?"

Hearing the final demand, Augusta nodded with a yes reply as if Roz could actually see her and disconnected the line.

DECISION MADE

Even before he opened the door to his suite of offices, Sheriff Joe Jackson heard Roz's voice and detected urgency. His day had started, as it always started, before dawn at the Buns Up Bakery. The townsfolk referred to it as the Buns and it was the only bakery and coffee shop in Oresville, a small town in the central Colorado Rockies with a population just shy of 2,000. If you were born and raised in Oresville, you got a kick out of calling it Becky's Buns because the owner was a local gal, second generation, Rebecca Riney.

Joe was looking forward to the start of his annual holiday vacation to finish out the calendar year. He held tight to this personal tradition and always took the last week and a half of every year as vacation. This started years ago when his four daughters were young and his wife, Mary Margaret, or as he liked to call her my Sweet M&M, needed help with the holiday planning and policing their kiddos who were only three years apart. Joe's full-time help in the last days of the year was Sweet M&M's *sanity requirement*.

Joe graduated from the local high school a year before Mary Margaret where they were the proverbial "high school sweethearts." He had a football scholarship for college in the big city of Denver. Unfortunately, the promising football career lasted only a month before a permanent knee injury canceled the football career and the free money for tuition that came with it. He stayed on to complete his freshman year, waiting for her to catch up after she graduated high school, a year behind him.

Summer passed and Mary Margaret moved out of Oresville to join Joe in Denver. Their new found freedom and the raging hormones for the teenage sweethearts quickly became out of control. With the event of an unplanned family looming, they dropped out of college, moved back to their beloved hometown, and quickly got married. Daughter number one arrived and neither of them was old enough to vote, let alone be parents. Just as Joe turned twenty-one, twin daughters numbers two and three were demanding feedings every four hours and daughter number four was due before Thanksgiving.

At the age of nineteen, Joe had gotten hired as a janitor with a small basement office in what was then the new Green County Office Building. He finished his college undergraduate program over a seven-year period and moved from the basement to Deputy Sheriff on the first floor. Ten years later the current Sheriff unexpectedly died in what was deemed a questionable, unseemly circumstance. Joe was appointed to the Acting Sheriff position by the county commissioners.

Enjoying his position in law enforcement, he became adept at campaigning every election season and the months in between. Fast forward twenty some years and he still liked to campaign, but now it was a full-time occupation. He had crossed to the dark side of law enforcement as an elected politician. He was still reminding people that he had worked his way up the ladder from the basement. To sweeten the pitch, he always added that a 'good ol' local boy' for sheriff was the best way to go and the voters agreed.

Sheriff Joe had entered his suite of offices with a grand sweep of the front door, a long stride into the reception area, and a slight hesitation similar to a pose in case there should be a camera waiting on the other side of the door. He was always practicing for re-election and entrance into a room demanded confidence or the look of being *in charge*.

"Whoa! What's all the yelling about, Roz? I could hear ya in the hallway." Joe's voice carried the calmness of reason. His only tell of concern was when he reached up to his left ear and gave the lobe a little tug. His voice seemed to flow naturally from his size thirteen cowboy boots to his 'high and tight' standard haircut atop his six foot plus frame. His modulated voice magically carried a good distance without being raised a single decibel and had been perfected over the years, steady and reassuring, thanks to his crowded home life. The sound level at the two-bedroom one bath bungalow was often at the maximum level of endurance for human ears without ear protection. Four daughters only a few years apart called for a calm, readily identifiable voice from at least one parent.

The question he asked was ignored or never heard by Roz who was multitasking as only Roz could do. The experts in productivity, who have tried to prove time and again that multitasking is worthless, have never seen Rosalind Marie Beaudreau in high gear. She was mentally running through a checklist, mumbling an agreement, grabbing for the desk phone, her other hand flipping through the cards of the old Rolodex file, locating the Green County Search & Rescue number, dialing it, and trying to explain the circumstances to Joe—all at the same time. Her messy bun of dark wavy hair had come undone and the grim set to her face was all business, no time for proper greeting of the boss.

In her special emergency staccato voice she announced, "Augusta's up above Azure Lakes. There's a pickup off the trail, hung up on trees, almost buried in the snow from yesterday's storm. A person appears to be in the driver's seat, unmoving, maybe dead or worse. I'm calling the search team right now to get them moving and here are the GPS coordinates for you."

Maybe dead or worse? How can anyone be maybe worse than dead? Joe wondered as he took the note from Roz. Using the ultimate in a soothing, all-knowing voice, "Sounds like No Name Gulch. What's Augusta doin' up there by herself?" Joe's renowned textbook knowledge of the area came from a lifetime in the town of Oresville with the exception of the fourteen months he spent attending college down in Denver thirty years ago.

"She's not by herself. She's out with the Gettin' Higher Snowmobile Club and Queennie is with her. Remember her?"

Joe was staring at Roz trying to place this Queennie person. He knew by name or face every voter in Green County, but Queennie must have been from a different county, likely a visitor. He started to pull on his left ear, raised his eyebrows in concentration mode, and offered, "Can't place that one."

Typical man only remembers what will make a difference to him. Roz rushed on, not waiting for the Sheriff to figure it out, "Well, whatever, Queennie is there too and the usual assortment of snowmobile club people."

Still stuck on trying to place this potential voter, Joe gave up and moved on. "Well, thank God Augusta's not by herself, but I wouldn't put it past her. The pickup must have gone off the road yesterday during the storm if snow is covering it. So what would anyone be doing up there in such

15

crazy weather when the storm was indisputably predicted for days? It was a doozy, the whole nine yards—howling winds, bitter cold temps. It'd be a real wonder if anyone survived that mess."

Joe was rationalizing between going up there just to see something off the road or staying in the office, passing time, waiting for his vacation to start at twelve noon sharp. On the other hand, he never missed an opportunity for the citizens of Green County to see their sheriff in action. He was speculating there could be a photo opportunity if Garcia, the local newspaper's editor, would send up his reporter, Carrie Jean. He could feel his noon start of vacation drift into the thin air at Oresville's nearly 10,500 feet above sea level. With that thought, he decided a drive up the mountain trail would be the right thing to do.

COURT ON HOLD

While Roz was talking to the search team, Joe decided to call in his lead deputy, Phoebe Korneal, who worked the two to ten shift on patrol and served as the county's as needed detective for the occasional serious crime. She was always ready to practice the detecting skills when called.

Joe was thinking, *Phoebe's the right person whether it is just a vehicle off the road or something more dire. She'll be on duty throughout the holidays to keep an eye on the results. Her dedication and thoroughness guarantee my vacation will remain intact. Joe silently hoped this wasn't the result of some local kid with a new driver's license who had not bothered to listen to the weather forecast.*

Phoebe had come to Oresville several years ago directly from the Salt Lake City Police Department where her law enforcement career began. Even with a few years of in-depth patrol experience and training as a detective, the odds of her landing a permanent assignment to Major Crimes? Slim to none. A career in patrol? Not her goal. She had higher hopes.

In addition, Phoebe's personal life was shattered when the love of her life ran off with her golfing partner who was also, supposedly, a best friend. It turned out that this girlfriend was a better, closer friend to Phoebe's boyfriend. At that point, Phoebe renamed Salt Lake City to SL-ICK with the "ICK" emphasized.

This romantic disaster and the lack of career opportunities were enough to send Phoebe in search of a new job in a new location, where she could heal in the security of a new community around new people. Maybe she would find that dream job in a new location. After a few years in her slightly used rented trailer, she had not healed that memory or even attempted to do so. Her work kept her on patrol most of the time, but she did get the occasional opportunity to exercise her detective skills.

A distrust of men in general still smoldered, tamped down deep in her brain's limbic system. In its place, she had developed a slight register on the OCD scale. This helped to keep everything on the surface of her life organized, properly placed, and tightly wrapped. Without the interference of emotions involving *relationships with the opposite sex,* Phoebe appeared to be content.

Her best friend from the old neighborhood in Salt Lake City, Carrie Jean O'Brien, was already living in Oresville at the time of the Salt Lake City Relationship Disaster. When Phoebe announced that she intended to leave SL-ICK come hell or high water, Carrie Jean was certain that Phoebe needed the thin air of Colorado to get her life straightened out. With a stubbornness to match her fiery red hair, Carrie Jean started campaigning to convince Phoebe to move to Oresville. There happened to be an opening in the Sheriff's office for a patrol deputy. It would be the perfect location to start anew. Carrie Jean had already convinced her step-brother, Bill Diamond, to come to Oresville, where he now served as the Undersheriff of Green County. The old neighborhood would be back together again if she could just convince Phoebe to come to Oresville—Carrie Jean, Phoebe, and Bill.

As he sat down at his desk, Sheriff Joe hit the speed dial on his office phone calling Phoebe, "Sorry to bother you like this, but it looks like we have a truck off the trail below Slide Lake. We might have a dead body or worse. I need you to start work this morning before your normal schedule with a little overtime pay. Can you come to the office and we'll drive up to the area together? Let's call it a possibility to brush up on your detective skills."

Phoebe was listening closely and started the run of a million and one questions beginning with where exactly is this Slide Lake. She took a deep breath and waited.

"I'll fill you in on what I know when you get here." Joe was thinking, *I might be able to save the start of my vacation after all.*

Phoebe could always use a few hours of overtime to pad her bank account and the idea of a *dead body or worse* brought out her detective instincts. Using overtime instead of a higher paying detective position, the Sheriff's budget maintained its perfect balance to the dollar. Besides, there was probably not enough crime in Green County to warrant such a position. Last summer she had investigated the passing of Old Al Lewis, a gold prospector in the mountains surrounding Oresville. It had taken extra work, heavy on the case management, but she handled it smoothly from beginning to a quick end in less than a week. Despite her rather rusty detective skills, the overtime for some detective work on a case would be sweet. A new schedule for patrol was starting on the first of January and Phoebe was switching to the morning shift, six to two in the afternoon. Additionally, she was carefully supporting the more twenty-first century approach to scheduling with four ten-hour days. Often overtime could have been avoided if the department's scheduling for its officers was a standard ten-hour shift, four days a week.

This approach had little traction with Sheriff Joe whose conservative view was a solid, "If it ain't broke, don't fix it." As a balance to this theory, Phoebe was building a case for the ten hour shifts as a way to save money in the budget and she offered to take over managing the schedule each month. The 'tipping point' for support was the fact that it was Joe's idea to begin with or so he was led to believe.

"No problem, Sheriff, I can use the overtime." Phoebe was sounding eager while trying to visualize something worse than a dead body.

"It'll take a few minutes to tidy up and get dressed. I'll meet you in the parking lot, say in about twenty-six minutes. Got it?"

While she was reassuring him, she'd be there as fast as possible and visualizing a *dead or worse* possibility, a little voice behind her was speaking, *Drive up to Slide Lake in the heavy snow from yesterday? This sounds like pure nonsense. Even the super-duper Sheriff's pride and joy, a Jeep Wrangler, would have problems in several feet of new snow. That area is above eleven thousand feet in elevation and the snow never melts until June or July. Trusting him to drive them up the mountain was a real challenge for her, or for that matter, trusting any man.*

She threw in, "Hey, Sheriff, with the big storm yesterday I wonder about trying to drive up there? You know the terrain well enough to get us there for sure, but what about callin' out the snowcat machine for this one?" She went on in a serious, businesslike, deputy sheriff voice,

"It'd be good practice even if we don't need all that power, ya know?"

Silence on the other end. Holding her breath, she could tell he was mulling over this suggestion.

After a few minutes, the sheriff came back, "Phoebe, I was just thinking the same thing myself. My cousin runs the motor vehicle and safety department for the mining company. I'll give Cousin George Jackson a quick call. See ya shortly. And thanks, Phoebe."

Having weighed in on the dead or worse description, she concluded an opportunity could be at hand and chuckled to herself, *This could be the break I need for a full-time detective spot and the new business cards would read, Phoebe Korneal, Detective, Green County, Colorado. Hum, no. Lead Detective, Green County Sheriff, Colorado. Hum, no. Green County Sheriff's Only Detective. Hum, no. Well, whatever, I can play with the appropriate wording on the way.*

She filled up the thermos with strong, black, French Roast, the current favorite. With some angst, the kitchen disposable mop and cleaning spray were set aside to wait for the daily unnecessary cleaning—not her style to leave anything incomplete. Living by herself and working full time hardly required daily purification, but most certainly as soon as she returned home tonight, her daily cleaning regimen would be completed. Phoebe was making a concerted effort to not be so obsessive about her lifestyle while practicing a new mantra allowing for flexibility—*A clean place for everything and everything MOSTLY in its place.*

Feeling good about leaving a bit of disorder, she practically skipped down the hallway to the bedroom. Getting ready for a full day of work required just a quick, haphazard brush through her long, chestnut hair, pulling it into an instant ponytail at her lower hairline. She pulled on her bulletproof vest over two layers of warm shirts, added the thirty-plus pound duty belt, and stuck her cell phone into a pocket. After lacing up her weatherproof Columbia snow boots, donning a fur lined Aviator's cap and a *Michelin Man* full length down filled coat, her five-foot ten-inch frame was surrounded in a cocoon of warmth for a day in the mountains.

The final stop before exiting her rented single-wide trailer was the gun safe. She unlocked it and added the gun to the duty belt. The trusty Glock 22 was compact, reliable, and had little chance of a misfire. At the front door she hesitated, thinking, *I really should put away the mop and pail.* After a half beat, she admonished herself, *No! It can wait 'til I get back.* She definitely thought this was some progress on the OCD thing.

Phoebe always referred to her single wide house trailer as *rented.* It was a proper reference when she first moved in several years ago. She told friends and family that she had to be ready to move fast should the planets align. Rented housing would be easy to vacate in the event of opportunity, local or not. In the years she had lived at The

Court, the rent had not been increased one single dollar. The stingy owner of the Tiny Town Mobile Home Court valued having a deputy sheriff in residence, thereby saving the expense of a professionally designed security system. Even though Phoebe's single-wide dated back to the early '70s, it had none of the typical accoutrements expected of a vintage trailer. The permanent residents at The Court littered their lots with sheds, lean-tos, and dog houses as needed. Her only enhancement was a single strand of Christmas lights around the front end of the trailer and she made every effort to plug them in on her evenings off. It was her one extravagance intended to brighten the rental.

Phoebe felt the bitter cold in spite of the milky morning sun trying to make a difference. She had to jerk hard to open the frozen door and quickly maneuvered into the seat of the silver Ford F-150, adjusting the layers of clothing and the bullet proof vest. Boobs and the vest were a constant struggle. The truck started up with little coaxing and Willie Nelson was blasting, "Good Hearted Woman." Unconsciously, she agreed with the name of the song, mentally snapped her fingers, checked her watch, and spoke over the music to no one in particular, "Perfect. Six minutes to the office and I'll be arriving at exactly the twenty-five-minute mark with one minute to spare for any unplanned interruption on the way. Way to go, Phoebe-girl. Right on time." So much for slacking on the obsessive thinking in her life. She slammed the gears into action and aimed the vehicle for town.

ANOTHER CHANCE

Pulling into the Sheriff's parking lot behind the county building, she could see the steam coming out of the exhaust pipe of the tricked-out Sheriff Department's Wrangler. Phoebe grabbed the coffee thermos, slid out of the pickup, paused to adjust clothing, vest, and boobs then hurried over to the Jeep. She was being careful not to slip on the icy, snow-packed ground. The lot had been somewhat cleared of the new snow and the SUVs and sedans had been neatly uncovered.

Newly hired Green County janitor, Mickey Walker, was standing with a sturdy snow broom, looking down at a bit of snow while trying to avoid direct eye contact with the Sheriff or anyone else in the vicinity.

Mickey worked the Sunday to Wednesday shift, ten hours each day. Snow removal was the constant focus all winter at this elevation and this young guy was a natural. He seemed shy, not the more gracious 'reserved' as a category. He looked to be in his early twenties and newly relocated to town from somewhere on the Front Range.

Joe was talking to him through the open driver's side window, "The parking lot's lookin' sharp, Mickey. I'd like you to make that a priority at the start of each morning through the winter. If you can make that happen, I'll be one happy camper."

The Sheriff liked to have his department fleet ready to roll first thing every day—clear of snow was a productivity enhancement. Joe remembered back in the day when he worked patrol. Snow removal from an assigned vehicle was always a great time to share happenings and get caught up with fellow officers. If the removal took long enough, one could segue directly into the morning coffee break from the parking lot and it would easily be ten in the morning before serious law enforcement work would begin. He was no dummy. Been there, done that.

Mickey was nodding like he was listening, but gazing off to Mount Massive. He was starting a career at the county like Sheriff Joe had started, in the basement as a janitor. So far, he was a hard worker. After less than a month he was still trying to get his bearings on what the job required including what was not listed in the job description.

Phoebe took in all this as she neared the Wrangler. She gave a quick nod of greeting to Mickey and turned to Joe, a note of anxiety in her voice. "What's goin' on here?"

"All I can tell you is Augusta and her snowmobile buddies were trying out their machines on the new snow up around No Name Gulch below Slide Lake. Anyway, they spotted this red truck off the trail, barely hangin' on its side, supported by the big pines up there. They can't get to it. The ditch is too steep to ride down on their machines and too dangerous to walk. They said it looks like someone's in the front seat."

Quickly turning this over in her mind, Phoebe questioned a possibility, "Are they sure it's a body? Could it be just some other debris looking like a person?"

Overhearing this official Sheriff business talk, Mickey quickly turned and walked away from the conversation. He seemed keen on eliminating every possible flake with a renewed urgency in his sweeping of the snow packed parking lot. Joe was watching the young guy's efforts and seemed impressed with this new hire. He continued the update. "Good point. It's partially covered in snow from yesterday's storm. I'll bet the winds up there at tree line are whippin' enough to maybe see the outline of a person or thing in the driver's seat. We'll know more when we get up there—the sooner the better."

Joe hesitated, judging the work the new hire was doing. He was satisfied with the kid's progress and continued, "Roz notified the search and rescue group and

31

the fire chief says the volunteers are coming together. With all this new snow it'll be tough goin', but they're gettin' out their big two-passenger snowmobiles. We'll meet where the snow plowing ends near the Azure Lakes. Meanwhile, Cousin George is onboard, bringing the mine's snowcat machine to the rendezvous location."

Green County had a handshake agreement with the Moly Mine to use their heavy duty, six passenger snowcat as needed. It was quite the machine and could handle anything the mountains could hand out.

Phoebe was looking at Joe and thinking ahead with the mention of the snowcat. *What if Joe or I had to drive it? I'm a fast learner. Is my ego speaking here? If Joe were to drive, we'd be all day just to get to the site. Back in Utah the snowcat had a standard shift, several extra low granny gears for the tough stuff, four articulating tracks, and were equipped with sturdy five-point seat belt harnesses just in case it flipped. I could handle that.* Her confidence was renewed.

Eager to get to the meeting point, Joe hurried on, "I suspect they'll be at the rendezvous site when we arrive, if we aren't too late. I'll drive us, so saddle up."

Phoebe did a finger snap and ended with a pointer to Joe, "Right." Then she did a quick check around the parking lot and rounded the back of the Jeep to the passenger side. She preferred to drive but sensed that Sheriff Joe was already done with that conversation.

Mickey was doing a great job of sweeping as a special finishing touch. He seemed to be keeping one eye on them and Phoebe had a gut feeling he wanted to talk. Probably just a "newbie" question. They had to get moving. Phoebe made a mental note to try to find him later. Helping the new hires sometimes paid off down the road.

The Sheriff's department ran on a slim force these last two weeks of the year to allow for as much family time as possible. Law enforcement demands were traditionally lighter this time of the year. Being single, Phoebe was always willing to help the family guys by working overtime and trading shifts. With the notable absence of a social life, she had decided a better schedule was called for. In January, she was looking forward to not only the fresh start of a new year, but also the favored 6 a.m. to 2 p.m. shift. *Time to get a life, Phoebe-girl.*

UP WE GO

It was a quiet Tuesday morning in Oresville. The sky was a deep blue that had no memory of yesterday's storm. The blizzard had brought in much needed snow and the dirt roads and trails at higher elevations were finally covered with a thick slab. In some areas the depth had reached as much as four feet of the white stuff. At over ten thousand feet in elevation, the town had gotten a foot, all powder resulting in the recording of very little moisture. The winds were calm and this made the mid-teen temperatures in town tolerable. The December sun held no promise of doing much to help with the cold air.

A county worker had plowed the town's roads already this morning. The snow was somewhat packed down from yesterday's storm. This encouraged people to stay home, out of the way of the town's novice drivers. School was out until after the New Year so the teenagers would drive around this morning, noon and night looking for something to do. The auto crash rate always skyrocketed with the magic formula of snow and teens learning to drive on the stuff. Add to this the fact that Christmas was only two days away, traffic for last minute shoppers had hit an anxiety level higher than neighboring Mt. Massive at 14,429 feet above sea level. It all added up to a recipe for disaster.

Like any small town, kids learning to drive were part of the fabric that builds community. The residents gave a knowing glance with a tolerant nod to one another whenever a near miss occurred and the incident was shared at the Buns over coffee.

This snow combined with the urgency to get shopping completed was the perfect storm for the local and only city cop, Onis Adams. His ticket book was in place, ready with fresh pages, for some end of the year income for the town. Billy Baldwin, owner of Green County Towing and Recovery Service, had his tow trucks idling, ready for calls to the mishaps that were bound to happen with the first snow of the season.

Once inside the Jeep, Sheriff Joe added, "Phoebe, thanks for dropping everything to start early and help me out, and for always being so prompt. I can count on you, especially when things might go south on a callout."

Phoebe nodded in acknowledgement while looking out the window of the Jeep checking the storefronts, always on alert.

"As you know, today I start vacation and I'm out of the office for the rest of the year. The news of this mishap could mess with my vacation plans. Undersheriff Diamond will be in charge of the office, but I'll need you to be the lead on this incident. It's probably just bad driving combined with no common sense. Case closed."

Was the Sheriff whining? "Of course," she assured him. "Enjoy Christmas vacation with your family. I've got this." She was always ready to remind Sheriff Joe that she had the skills he needed for the department.

Coming out of the parking lot, Joe gunned the engine and the Jeep fishtailed. He smiled wide and wrestled it to the correct side of the street. He was in his element. They went to Main Street, made a left turn and roared out of town toward the cutoff to Slide Lake and the meeting point.

"Don't worry. I'll take care of this accident or otherwise." *Maybe I'll make detective yet.*

Then she added, "Sounds like we could have unique circumstances here. If it turns out there really is a body in the front seat, we might go from a routine mishap to a dead body investigation. My top-notch detective skills, training, and experience will be required. Hope the area won't be too compromised before we get there. It's been awhile since I've had any sleuthing to do. Actually, it was

37

back at the end of August when Old Al died." Every opening she could create she liked to remind Joe of the outstanding work on a recent case. Not really bragging, just a steady reminder of her professionalism.

"That's been months now, Phoebe." Then he quickly added, "You did a mighty fine job on that deal with Old Al. Had it not been for your doubts about the cause of his death, we would have assumed he died because he was, well, old. You know just natural causes at the ripe old age of 69. Like metal fatigue on an airplane, the old body just wears out." With this thinking Joe let out a bit of a chuckle at this most astute observation. He continued, "Who would have thought about arsenic poisoning for someone living in the great outdoors?" There was a long pause while he switched gears then finished with, "How time flies. Hard to believe it's the end of another year already."

Phoebe was not listening to Joe's comments. She was stuck on the thought of these end-of-year holidays. "Yes, Christmas again," trying to maintain an upbeat, holiday-like voice. To herself she thought, *And I'm still alone, with no prospects of that changing, still living in a rented trailer, with no prospects of that changing and still shooting for a detective position with no prospects, period. What's wrong with me? Maybe next year I should take the leap and get a dog.*

As Joe drove the Jeep toward the meet point, Phoebe continued her reminiscing. *I love Christmas with friends in Oresville, but there's an empty place nagging at me, the one I can't seem to fill. It's been that way since the SL-ICK Disaster some people would call a relationship. Oh, wait. What about Ponytail Guy, Bart? He has potential in all of this thinking. He's the first guy in years that I've been interested in. Hmmm.*

Snapping out of her reverie with the thought of Bart, aka Beautiful Man, she smiled. Her focus re-centered as they pulled up to the congregation of search and rescue volunteers. Joe parked the Jeep as close as possible to their machines without getting in the way. They slid out of it and joined the assortment of grim-faced volunteers. The snowcat was there, idling. George was pacing in his XXL snowmobile suit anxious to get the show on the road.

He was not only a confirmed biological cousin of Sheriff Joe Jackson, but also a cousin to nearly half of the assembled crew of volunteers. His mom, dad, step-whatevers and an assortment of distant and suspected family members would send a skilled genealogist into cardiac arrest just trying to diagram how he came by a title of *cousin*. To save time on useless discussion, the townsfolk of Oresville called him Cousin George and skipped over the intricacies of said title.

His birth certificate read, George Andrew Jackson. He was named after the first one who was born back in the 1800s. In 1858, the first George arrived in Colorado after an uneventful few years' prospecting during the California Gold Rush. A skilled outdoorsman and a hobby prospector, he preferred "working" in the great outdoors to counting beans in a local general store. In the deep of winter, January, 1859, he was camping and hunting in an area known today as Idaho Springs, and used his empty coffee cup to pan a few cups of gravel. He got a few worthless flakes and then a gold nugget. This was what would be called the first *real gold discovery* and sparked the fever for the short-lived Colorado Gold Rush.

A third or fourth generation later, George was following in the footsteps of this possible ancestor from Colorado's history. He was a natural fit as Safety Director for the Moly Mine, short for molybdenum, and number forty-two on the periodic table. The mine owned the huge snowcat machine and George loved showing off his driving skills at the slightest opportunity. He routinely monitored the fire department channel used for search and rescue demands. When his cousin, Sheriff Joe, called him this morning for assistance, the snowcat was already being pulled through town on its trailer in the direction of the meeting point just short of the Azure Lakes.

George was faking a smile as a greeting, "Hey guys, thought you'd never get here. Did you stop at Becky's Buns for coffee? Even Carrie Jean beat you up here."

"Never mind. Let's hit it," Joe shot back with a matching fake smile. He gave his left ear a slight tug, and turned to Carrie Jean. "I didn't have time to call your boss, Garcia. How'd it happen that you're here before us?"

"Hey, Joe. Hi, Phoebe-girl. Now Sheriff, you know Augusta would call me first. I'm surprised to see you here so fast." After a two second pause, "Not," was added under her breath. All of the search personnel of the Green County Search and Rescue were ready to go, just waiting for the Sheriff's Department to arrive. Carrie Jean had to rub it in. Anxious to get to the accident scene and record the details, she mumbled to herself, "Dollar waitin' on a dime."

Standing in the cold, Carrie Jean was wrapped in her warmest black full-length down-filled coat, matching ski pants, hiking boots, gloves, and an oversized knit beanie for her huge amount of red hair. It seemed to be popping out from the edges like an explosion beneath the cap. Not listening for her answer to his question, Sheriff Joe was already walking towards the snowcat.

Carrie Jean had a long history of practicing for an occupation as a newspaper ace. She was inquisitive by nature and nosy enough to always seek the sordid details of any situation, even if she had to loosely suggest "something more" as a backstory. Adding her smartphone pics for the 'picture is worth a thousand words' angle, Carrie Jean kept the citizens of Oresville up-to-date with local happenings. Her boss, Jesus Garcia, had added an online news brief called the High Country e-Blast! with a deadline of twelve o'clock noon most days of the week. This product became Carrie Jean's and she fully embraced the ownership for the e-Blast!

Calling herself the Ace Reporter for the High Country Gazette, she had many coveted bylines to her credit to substantiate the "Ace" title. This came easily as she was the only employee of the paper.

Garcia was officially the editor-in-chief and he had taken Carrie Jean under his wing and trained her in the finer points of mostly honest reporting, or enhancing the news based on the facts as were sometimes suggested. The same family had owned the Gazette for over a hundred years and Garcia had married a daughter of the family a few years back. When not in a public setting, Carrie Jean liked to tease him, "This makes you the owner-editor by the default of marriage."

Phoebe offered a fist bump to CJ, a nod to George, and they hustled after Sheriff Joe who was nearing the snowcat. George pointed to the back seat for Phoebe and Carrie Jean as he continued to the driver's seat.

Joe would not be expected to drive the machine and Phoebe would not have to learn how to drive it, as she had worried at the start of this call out. The Sheriff was a careful driver but too slow for Phoebe's satisfaction. If they were riding together, Phoebe had learned to volunteer as the driver, ". . . to give you a well-deserved break, Sheriff." Joe usually took the bait and welcomed the chance to sit back and appreciate the views at 10-5 as he was chauffeured about Green County.

Phoebe smiled to herself as she observed CJ dressed appropriately in "let's go for a ride in the mountains in zero-degree weather" attire. *CJ looks like a moving fireplug.* Carrie Jean was barely five foot tall and casual would be a fair descriptor of her typical style. The cat was higher than she was tall and she struggled with her short frame to enter the vehicle. Phoebe gave CJ a boost, propelling her into a seat and then stepped to the other side. With long legs, Phoebe easily stepped up into the backseat. They were ready to depart.

The search and rescue volunteers were on their snowmobiles and had roared up the trail while the snowcat was being readied. They were in hot pursuit of the Gettin' Higher Snowmobile Club at the emergency location. These Green County Fire Department volunteers were a tight knit, highly trained team of fifteen people who were skilled in the art and science of rescue. This announcement of a vehicle off the road was the first call of the season and surely would test their mountain terrain rescue abilities. Each of them expected every emergency summons would be a search and rescue, as opposed to the sad process of recovery when all hope was lost.

The giant snowcat followed the path created by all the snowmobile activity. The snow was noticeably deeper off to each side of the path. The winds seemed to be lessening and the winter sun, weak at this altitude, did little to create warmth. A backdrop of cloudless, light blue sky promised hours of decent weather for the morning albeit cold with temperatures at zero or below.

Inside the machine, the passengers were each tightly bound in place with the five-point seat belt harnesses doing their job. The noise in the cab prevented the occupants from talking and each was anticipating what they would find up there. George stopped the snowcat just short of the area where the Gettin' Higher Club was gathered. Augusta's group had moved their machines to the far side of the road and above the staging area, leaving room for the snowcat to park. The search and rescue team had easy access to the vehicle which was braced against the tall, snow-covered, lodgepole pines down in the gulch. The county volunteers were already in action for the rescue side of the equation.

OFF THE ROAD

A s the snowcat pulled to a stop where the volunteers were gathered, Phoebe could see just the top of the red pickup. The rest of it was covered with snow. Hindered with all her extra padding, she clumsily shifted in her seat, working to slide out of the snowcat as quickly as possible. With a giant push, she bounded out of the cab and promptly sank to her knees in the deep, powdery snow. Frustrated, she let out a surprised yell, "What the hell?"

George came to her aid waving his hand which held a pair of snowshoes, "Hey, Phoebe, wait a minute, here come the snowshoes to your rescue."

"Perfect, I didn't even think to bring mine. Thanks." She put them on, clumsily shifted her vest into a better position, straightened the heavy-duty belt, and pulled out the cell phone. Standing tall and snapping pictures from the edge of the road where the rescue team was setting up, she was capturing the action as best possible under the circumstances. There were tracks from today's snowmobiles, but nothing leading to the truck or from the road to the truck. Any hope of tracking how the truck ended up off the road was fading as the action intensified.

Carrie Jean found her multiple layers of warm clothing added a challenge for her as she attempted a graceful egress from the confined quarters of the snowcat. She was hesitating to exit into the deep snow, knowing she would sink up to her butt. "Cousin George, where are you?" She was frantically eye-balling the snow as she saw the hot news of the day vaporizing without photos and interviews.

George came to the rescue. Carrie Jean sighed with relief as he offered a pair of snowshoes and helped put them on as she sat sideways. He was a giant of a person at nearly seven feet tall, with a solid muscular frame to match. Once the snowshoes were on Carrie Jean's boots, he lifted her out like a doll. "You're on your own now CJ. Good luck."

He left her to figure out the rest for herself and with long strides stepped over to help the rescue effort. *Safety First* was always on his mind. He did not want to be part of instigating another mishap.

Sheriff Joe seemed to instinctively know what was required as the snowcat came to a stop. With the snowshoes already attached, he cautiously slid out of the 'cat and stepped to the volunteers. Like the motor memory skill of riding a bicycle he automatically slipped into snowshoe mode raising his knees enough to clear a path for the awkward paddles on each foot. The search team was pulling out the rescue equipment, getting everything set up with no discussion except for a single word here or there.

"How can I help?" he offered in his calm, reassuring voice.

Someone heard him and nodded back, "We've got this. Let's have the club members stand down, out of the way for now."

Sheriff Joe tugged on his left ear and pressed his lips into "grim mode" indicating to the speaker he would get out of their way. This was an opportunity to acknowledge the citizens who voted for a Sheriff every few years. He assumed a serious, all-business look and did a snowshoe side step over to where the group had gathered intent on shaking hands all around. Maybe posing for a photo should the opportunity present itself.

Working the snowshoes, Carrie Jean intended to head towards the rescue team. While most people lift their knees enough to get a lighter step on the snowshoes. At barely five foot tall, she looked more like a Lipizzaner Stallion, prancing and bucking to operate the paraphernalia on her boots. The bystanders noticed the flailing, high-stepping, occasional grunting of indistinguishable cuss words, and worked hard to contain their laughter. No one offered to carry her to a final standing spot.

THE LAST SLIDE

Stopping just short of the rescue team, she took a deep breath and wiped the sweat from her forehead. A round of applause rose up from the observation position of the snowmobile club. She took a slight bow to this acknowledgement and directed her attention to any tidbits she could use for the daily e-Blast! Her livelihood depended on a daily headline via the use of a cell phone permanently set to the Record App. This enabled a recap of the action for the twelve-noon deadline.

The e-Blast! was the daily newsletter distributed electronically at twelve noon sharp, five days each week. It carried any local happenings since yesterday's banner even if it was nothing more than temperature changes, barometric pressure updates, and wind speeds. The actual newspaper was printed every week on Thursday for a Friday distribution as had been the practice for over one hundred years.

The local newspaper was just as important today as it was in the 1800s when the nation was in its infancy and the western states were being settled. Today national and world news is within reach electronically for anyone interested enough to put forth a bit of effort with cell phone apps. Local libraries are still the free repository of information along with the usual TV and radio news talking heads. The local news for any community is hard to come by and newspapers fill the void with printed and electronic media. With little staff and long hours, they keep the happenings of school teams in the limelight, town councils accountable, local clubs supported, and police reports hold the citizens hostage. The Oresville paper awards a Speed Demon of the Week on page two which is the first thing read every Friday.

Standing at the edge of the Wurtz Ditch Road, the members of the Gettin' Higher Snowmobile Club looked like a pack of meerkats focused on various elements of arrivals, law enforcement action, and rescue or recovery. They were hoping and speculating for any sign of life in the red truck. Snowmobile rides at high altitudes in winter were comfortable in full coverage bodysuits. Unfortunately, no St. Bernard dogs were available, so the high-end liquor was carried in backpacks along with assorted snacks—just because.

Being the first snowmobile ride for Queennie, Augusta was teaching her the intricacies of maneuvering the machine. All instructions were easily absorbed as Queennie had a natural affinity for vehicles thanks to a dad who was willing to teach his daughter how to manage just about any kind of machine and what made them tick. In town, her machine of choice was a Harley, but it required decent roads and fair weather. Not so good on snowy, mountain trails. Standing together, sipping out of thermal coffee mugs, they watched the action unfold in the gulch, and critiqued the efforts of the volunteers.

The two women, Augusta and Queennie, had become friends over the few months since Queennie's husband, Albert Lewis, had died unexpectedly. Old Al, as he was known because he was, well, old, was a rather informal business partner with Augusta. She was his winter landlord and let him stay in her family's homestead cabin in the mountains above Oresville. Every fall he would stop panning for gold. Taking his pet mule, Rose, with him, of course, he would move into the Higgins Cabin—rent free.

Theirs was a complimentary arrangement. Al needed shelter through the winters. Augusta needed someone to take care of the family cabin. It had been built by Augusta's great grandpa Higgins in 1860 at the start of the Colorado Gold Rush. Al was also coining his gold from each summer's prospecting using the Higgins apparatus tucked away at the family cabin. The smithing machinery used to turn the flakes and nuggets into gold coins dated back to the 1860s and great grandpa built it to be sturdy enough to run another hundred plus years —no planned obsolescence on this equipment.

Albert was an engineer at the Moly Mine until he discovered a largish gold nugget. Gold Fever hit hard and he quit his real job to roam the mountains around Oresville and the Arkansas Valley every summer for twenty-five plus years. Phoebe investigated his death and through a series of discussions and the help of Roz's research skills, the wife, Queennie, was discovered. Although they were not co-located as a married couple, Old Al continued to support Queennie over a period of nearly thirty years. Just before he passed, he had given her enough money to expand her radiator shop located in Pikeview on the Front Range of Colorado.

Augusta greeted Joe as he stepped to the small group, "Hey Joe, you remember Queennie, Old Al's wife?" She hurried on without bothering to remind Joe of the demise of Old Al, "Thanks much for this quick response. I could not believe how fast the search team got here. Queennie wanted to climb over the edge to get down to it and check for a person inside, but I convinced her to let the professionals do their jobs. No need to rescue another person."

Joe listened to this and added, "Right thinking on your part, Augusta. For a change." He took a second look at Queennie and it all clicked into place, not a voting member of this county.

Augusta added to his left-handed compliment, "We'll just stand guard, enjoy the scenery, and sip some of my homemade special tea, waitin' on the cavalry to save the day." She tipped her mug at the volunteers to indicate the cavalry she was talking about.

"I've perfected my tea to a winter infusion like a hot toddy but with my homebrew. We have an extra mug if you'd care to sample."

Sidetracked on the offer to sample the latest brew and not able to restrain himself, Joe took a deep breath and lectured, "Augusta, you and I have had this conversation about the unlawful production of liquor. It is not safe to drink with no protocols in place. Not to mention it's against the law."

"Now Joe, you're so right. We've had this conversation before, in fact many times, and you know my stand on it. My family has been in this valley for over a hundred and fifty years. The recipe has been perfected over the years and it's the property of the Higgins Family. With these two points, my recipe is therefore grandfathered in and I have every right to produce, use, and share. No sales involved and no taxes will ever be collected."

Joe had a look on his face similar to a bad odor wafting past his nose. This discussion was a no win for him.

As Phoebe shuffled over to the trio in her unwieldy snowshoes, she overheard the last part of the conversation. She knew instantly what she was walking into and chose to not get involved. When Augusta got on her high horse, it was better to get out of the way. Her picture taking continued from a new angle. At this stage, Phoebe was there as the lead patrol deputy. Detective status was not in play. She had best stick to the fact-gathering for her documentation.

She could not contain herself and let out a small chuckle at the overheard mention of Augusta's special tea. It was an alcoholic beverage that could be dangerous at this altitude of over eleven thousand feet, especially if consumed in copious amounts. "I'm not so sure about enjoying your tea early in the morning. But you're right, trying to reach that truck would be much too risky without proper equipment and backup. Good decision to call it in and then get out of the way."

The others in the club were sipping from their mugs and watching the pros work on rescue. If they were sampling Augusta's special tea, Phoebe was guessing there could be more impaired driving this morning than a truck going off the road. She stood with the Sheriff, Augusta, and Queennie and was comfortable in her swaddling of down. The snowshoes helped with navigation as long as no running was anticipated. The bright sun and now the absence of wind was a bonus.

If it were not for the seriousness of these circumstances, she could be enjoying this wintery view high in the Rockies. Just being at this altitude was refreshing and the killer view gold plated the morning. She was thinking she would drag out her snowboard this year and start using it again, with or without an escort. *I wonder if Beautiful Man would ski or board? Opps, don't overthink yourself, Girly-girl.*

As two volunteers made their way down the side of the gulch, two team members managed the ropes at the top. The rest of the observers stood quietly on the road's edge, watching in anticipation. Is there someone in the truck or not? Would this be a rescue, a recovery, or an abandoned pickup? They all hoped for the latter and had stopped talking, staying focused on the search and rescue team. The tension in the thin air was palpable.

George, the team coordinator, was especially attentive, watching the ropes and the men using them. The advance team of two carried the equipment needed for immediate use, along with a sled for rescue or recovery, as the case may be. Time was of the essence

Standing near George, Carrie Jean asked, "What are they going to do when they get to it?"

"First things first—they'll secure it and then immediately pop that door. There could be more at risk here than the obvious," George tersely replied.

Carrie Jean got the message and stopped questioning George. She let her recorder app on the phone continue to run, just in case he had something else to say.

Phoebe inched closer to the edge of the road being careful to stay out of the way and not fall down the side of the gulch. She was standing above where the team was quickly executing their plan and continued snapping photos as best as she could—her typical style of overkill.

Together, volunteers Nick and Jon trudged through the deep snow to the driver's side. They used ropes to secure it to the tall sturdy trees and checked both ends for a license plate number. Any little movement brought waves of snow falling from the pine branches above. Using the crowbar they had brought with them, they pried open the driver's side door and Nick tied it out of the way to a nearby tree.

Sheriff Joe was thinking about the start of his vacation. *How long will this delay go on? Hard to imagine that someone could have been up here trying to travel in yesterday's storm. It's probably just abandoned and Augusta and her great imagination brought us out here for a wild goose chase with the comment of maybe dead or worse. Having Phoebe along for the start of this case will help get me out of here sooner.* A yell brought Joe back to reality.

"There's a body in the front seat and a dog, too," an excited Jon called as they had their first look at the person. Meanwhile, a third member of the team rushed over the ridge to help Nick and Jon with the stretcher. Tension skyrocketed for those observing from the top. With the question of an abandoned truck resolved, now it was a question of rescue or recovery. The observers held their collective breaths, awaiting the verdict.

A large, black Labrador was holding its position sitting on the driver's lap and leaning against the chest of a woman who was not moving. The seatbelt had her secured behind the steering wheel. The lab started growling to prohibit entry and was frantically eyeing the snow, the volunteers swaddled in weather proof suits, and the people standing on the ridge. In one deft move, the dog seemed to think better of its plan and leaped from the front seat, promptly sinking to its flanks. So much for the growling as it struggled to jump above the snow, making for the Forest Service road above. The snowmobilers started yelling, trying to get its attention. Some of them were digging in backpacks for something to feed the dog.

Jon was the EMT for the rescue team on call for this shift. He went into action working to access her neck for a vitals assessment. The woman was not moving. Will there be a pulse or not? He peeled back her few layers of winter clothing and placed his fingers on her carotid artery, and called out to the waiting audience, "We've got a pulse. Very faint, but it's here."

The tension in the air cracked with a sudden, unified thought, "What can I do to help?"

Ticket to Ride

George immediately called out to a volunteer. "Gun it down the mountain till you get a signal on your cell and have dispatch to patch you through to Chance at Flight for Life. Have him meet us at our earlier meeting point above Azure Lakes. Tell him we have a female victim who has been in freezing cold at least overnight. She's unconscious with a faint pulse."

"I'm on it, George," responded the team member. "Do you have an ETA for the snowcat?"

"About half an hour, not more. Once we get this person up to the road and into the 'cat the downhill ride should be pretty quick."

Meanwhile, a third team member maneuvered down the slope to help Nick and Jon position the unconscious woman. Slowly and carefully, they moved her onto the heavy-duty sled that was designed for these less than desirable rescue operations. Strapping her down and covering her with two Mylar thermal blankets, they attached the necessary ropes to bring her out of the gulch. Two men were positioned at the top of the sled and one at the bottom as they worked to bring the sled up to the road. The stress of unexpected hope crackled in the cold, thin air.

Thanks to the encouragement of the snowmobilers, the dog had made it to the ledge and was lifted to the seat of a snowmobile. It was now shivering and whining with the indecision of eating the snacks offered or returning to its owner. Queennie sat next to the dog and tried to comfort it with a reassuring calm voice while everyone watched the rescue action, praying for the best.

The dispatcher for Flight for Life got the call and immediately contacted their number one and only pilot, Chance Watson. As a hobby helicopter owner and only pilot of an old American Bell UH-1 Huey, he lived for the occasional high drama of landing in precarious locations. The Rocky Mountains of Colorado were a natural draw. Chance was the well-earned nickname from a lifetime of risk. When he was "volun-told" to leave Alaska, he gladly joined his uncle, Doc Watson, in Oresville and arrived with a pile of early retirement money, two Army Ranger trained German Shepherds, and his pride and joy helicopter, affectionately referred to as "Belle". The intersection near Azure lakes where the volunteers and snowcat met earlier would be just the kind of challenge landing he lived for.

Further assessment of the woman would only delay the departure and was not necessary in the experience of the rescue team. Bad weather yesterday, off the road now, and unconscious with a weak pulse were the impetus for the next steps as the team steamrolled their operation.

Carrie Jean stood her ground, recording the events of the morning. Phoebe continued taking pictures of the scene. The club folks were taking care of the dog, and Sheriff Joe was thinking, *This might become a case for Phoebe's detective skills beyond routine patrol. My decision to bring her into the rescue was the right call.* He was reminded of the earlier comment, "a person maybe dead or worse." Now he was thinking, *this was the worse side of that equation.*

George had started the snowcat with the heater blasting and was organizing the ride back down the trail. He might need the Sheriff for anything official now that the event had escalated and ordered Joe to the cat. Phoebe would stay behind to investigate what little there was to see and take statements from the club members.

With the plans for carrying the woman in the snowcat, Carrie Jean figured she would be stranded. She snapped a last round of photos at the stretcher and the person bundled in it. It was quickly and smoothly being manhandled up the side of the gulch and onto the road. She could visualize her lead story already but needed to get nearer to a cell tower to make today's noon e-Blast! deadline. As the only person on staff for the newspaper, it was her job to meet the daily deadline, which she did consistently. She needed to hitch a ride and fast. With her snowshoes impeding quick movement, she shuffled over to a snowmobile and hunkered down hoping there would be room for her to hitch a ride back to her car.

Turning on her cell phone to record answers, Phoebe began asking questions of the Gettin' Higher club members who had spotted the truck. This accident could just be an unfortunate lapse in the driver's judgment. Having been called in as lead officer it was part of her job description to thoroughly investigate all aspects of a serious event. Serious was described as "Endangering the life or lives of all involved." This certainly fits the bill. Phoebe could swear she was hearing the noise of the helicopter in the distance already.

The stretcher-sled was hauled up the slope and whisked to the snowcat where Sheriff Joe and George were waiting alongside to assist in loading. The stretcher with the patient was placed and secured into the back half of the 'cat with Jon in attendance. He started an IV as standard operating procedure. George and Joe climbed into the front seats and off they went down toward Azure Lakes.

The search and rescue team always had at least one certified Emergency Medical Technician on every mobilization. The patient's vitals were continually monitored and recorded for future use when the team would do a thorough minute by minute review for training purposes. The fully loaded 'cat was carefully tracking down the mountain, minus the same passenger manifest it had carried earlier. The front seat passengers, George and Joe, were leaning forward in their seats as if they could urge the machine to move faster.

The trail at this point was snow-packed from all of the activity of the machines running up and down. There would be no melting until late spring at this altitude. Instead, layer upon layer of snow with each storm system would set up avalanche conditions.

Chance was bringing the helicopter into range of the broadcasted information from the EMT, Jon. As the Flight for Life pilot, he offered advice as to the nearest hospital helicopter pad for landing. In this case, the community hospital down the road was not an option because the landing site was under construction. They had gotten a ton of money from the government to expand their FFL landing zone. This dictated transport to the larger hospital in Pikeview, eighty miles away as the crow flies and the EMT would accompany the patient to the distant hospital.

At the site, Nick returned to the truck perched on the slope. Carefully entering through the open door, he quickly searched the passenger compartment and found the woman's handbag on the floor in front of the passenger seat. He put it inside his jacket and took a quick check behind the front seats. Nothing there. Using the ropes from the rescue operation, he pulled himself back up to the road.

Phoebe had been watching Nick and saw him retrieve something. "Whatcha' got there, Nick?" she asked as he topped the side of the gulch.

"Looks like a handbag of hers."

"Give it here and I'll secure it as evidence. Hopefully there'll be some ID in there and we'll notify any relatives. Thanks for a great job on this."

Phoebe looked around the area at the group of snowmobilers and rescue volunteers. "I think we're done up here for today. Let's sled it down the mountain and find out who this person is."

Carrie Jean was all about that. The sooner the better as she had the daily e-blast title page on the horizon already fixed in her mind's eye.

"Hey, CJ," called Augusta. "Hop on the back. I'll give you a ride down to your car."

"You bet. What about these damn snowshoes? I can hardly waddle wearing them."

"Come on over here and take them off. I'll tie 'em to the side of the machine and we can get them back to Cousin George."

Queennie chimed in. "Hey, Phoebe, there's plenty of room on my ride. Come on over. You can hold the dog and keep it company."

Wearing the thick winter gloves made the evidence bag awkward to handle and Phoebe's frustration was hitting the max level on the patience spectrum. She finally gave up and pulled off the gloves. Instantly her bare hands were freezing. The purse went into an evidence bag at lightning speed in the zero-degree weather and she tossed it onto Nick's snowmobile. He quickly placed the evidence bag into a compartment on the snowmobile and he was ready to go.

Phoebe was hesitant to ride anywhere with Queennie who was a seasoned motorcycle rider, always sans a helmet, but a newbie at snowmobiling. Plus, it was hard to tell how long they had been sampling Augusta's special hot tea. In Phoebe's law enforcement career, she had managed many episodes where these risk takers had become organ donors. She preferred a more cautious, seasoned driver.

Nick motioned to Queennie, "She can ride with me as we're both covered by the county's insurance plan." They all laughed at this, and Phoebe added, "Amazing how insurance makes decisions for us. But thanks for the offer, Queennie. I'll hang back and make sure we have everything covered. I don't want to come back up here if I can avoid it."

Phoebe looked at the dog and wondered what she could do with it. She had an earlier thought about getting a dog and quickly put that to the back of her mind. "How about you take the dog with you, Queennie, and we can worry about its future when we get back to town. Do we need to tie it down or something to make sure it stays?"

Queennie answered before the suggestion was complete. "Nope, dogs are better at balancing than most humans. It'll be fine."

Augusta heard that part of the conversation. "The dog's welcome to come to my house. I already have Al's mule in the front yard and she could probably use some company."

Augusta and Old Al's relationship had been strictly platonic. When he died of arsenic poisoning a few months ago, it became complicated when Al's estranged wife, Queennie, declared she wanted no part of Al's pet mule, Rose. Augusta had offered to keep her. Since Al's passing, Phoebe had heard the neighbors grumbling about the mule in the neighborhood.

To add to the emerging mess, this pack animal had taken a dislike to the mailman and ambushed the delivery person most days with spitting, loud noises, and aggressive movements. Augusta's relationship with the post office was checkered at best and the postmaster, Lyla Stoker, was threatening to stop delivery service to Augusta's home because of the animal. So far, no official complaint of "angry mule in the neighborhood" had been made to the town's cop, Onis Adams. Onis was the Oresville Magistrate, not a cop as he liked to remind people. There was a difference, but he would not specifically say what the difference was.

Onis was not keen on getting involved in neighborhood disputes and put the rumor mill regarding

Rose on the back burner. If he had his way, the whole town would be run by neighborhood homeowner associations and his job would be limited to writing parking tickets. The HOAs could deal with the Roses of this world. Planning to retire in March when he hit sixty-five, Onis decided to kick the can down the road. Let his replacement worry about the angry mule within city limits.

Hearing Augusta's comment, Phoebe reminded her, "You know there's an ordinance about keeping large animals and chickens in town. I'm pretty sure your neighbors aren't too happy."

"I haven't got time to listen to them complain, nor do I care much about the city's rules regarding the mule. Rose stays right where she is. My property, my life—Al's mule included. Besides, I was here first by several generations."

At this point, Phoebe decided to pick her losses and announced, "Then it's settled, you take the dog for now and I'll figure out where it belongs. Does it have a name?"

Queennie spoke up, "The tag reads Fido. Who names a dog Fido?"

Phoebe cracked a slight smile, shrugged her shoulders, thinking, *anyone with an attitude similar to Augusta's. My life, my rules, that's who.*

Augusta helped Carrie Jean get ready for the ride. The club members loaded up and formed a little caravan racing down the mountain road spinning a rooster's tail of snow in their wake.

Phoebe watched them move down the road and turned to Nick, "Thanks for the offer of the ride. Let's be sure to go last in case one of these club members has a mishap."

Nick added, "Good idea. I noticed they were all enjoying some kind of steaming drink."

With a small pause and a short laugh, she changed the subject. "What do you think happened here?"

"Hard to say, but with the bad weather yesterday, I'm thinking she just got disoriented. The storm was getting worse, she slid off the road, and luckily, she had the dog. It kept her warm and probably kept her alive. I noticed some damage to the back end. I suppose that happened when it went off the road. You'll know more when it gets towed to the yard."

"Yeah, we'll take a look. I'll call for the tow when we get down the hill."

The clouds were moving in across the mountain tops and the wind was picking up. The wind chill and temperatures were dropping. The rescue volunteers had carefully scanned the area for any trash from their operation, double checking for papers, empty water bottles, unused ropes and equipment. What was used to secure the scene would eventually be returned to the fire department by Billy Baldwin, the towing operator.

With the area cleaned to their satisfaction, the volunteers turned the machines around, and loaded up. Nick made sure his passenger, Phoebe, was safely tucked in for the short ride, and they roared down the trail in time for a late lunch.

What a morning, she was thinking as she heard the helicopter in the distance.

THE BIG REVEAL

When the snowcat reached the rendezvous site, the helicopter was one minute out. Chance could land on anything. The only consideration was incoming passenger's access to the side door of Belle. He expertly lowered the 'copter and awaited the EMT and patient. The sled with the woman was transferred into the helicopter and secured. Jon carried a Wilderness First Responder certification and was more than qualified to accompany the rescued woman to the hospital in Pikeview. As a WFR he had several years with the search and rescue team and had ridden with Chance many times. They seemed to share an unspoken language to do whatever was necessary to get their patient to the hospital.

THE LAST SLIDE

Sheriff Joe and George watched Belle take off amid a flurry of powdered snow drawn up by the powerful helicopter blades. Together they loaded the monster cat onto the trailer and it was ready to be towed back to the mine. Joe was already vacationing in his mind, but thought it best to wait for Phoebe to arrive. On the drive back to the office, they could discuss the next steps to determine what happened on the mountain.

Joe had seen it all over the years, first as a deputy and then as Sheriff. He was a native of Oresville and small-town living was his first and only choice for where to live. He and his Sweet M&M had never considered the possibility of moving to something bigger, more exciting, more options for their daughters, or additional temptations for career advancement. Mary Margaret was a teacher and in a few short years would be able to retire on her state-certified pension. Joe had toyed with the idea of retirement but could not see himself without county commissioner meetings, occasional mention in the local newspaper, greeting voters at Becky's Buns Up, or making sure his deputies were covering all the bases.

Now he had a great crew in place and between Undersheriff Bill Diamond and Phoebe as lead patrol, his job was reduced to the dark side of plain old politics. Phoebe was taking more and more responsibility and his idea of four ten hour shifts for each deputy was looking more and more feasible. He wondered where he had picked up the idea for it but it seemed a logical step and one that could save money on his budget.

Growing up in Oresville was exactly the life he wanted. A small town that was a real community where each person counted, regardless of contribution. The community pulled together to shoulder through whatever tough times or otherwise there might be. Every kid was doted on and in the school system was treated as above-average on the state testing regardless of their actual score. Everyone knew that the town's children would grow into their teen years and graduate high school. Only a few of these young adults would stay to become contributing citizens of Oresville. A small community is hard pressed to create opportunities for its youngest citizens.

As an only child, Joe, by default, was his parent's favorite bartender. They drank consistently, not constantly. As soon as he was old enough to safely pour milk from a carton, Joe Senior and Mom, Edna, taught him to be creative as the "family bartender in training." He was encouraged to make each concoction look delightful, with precise documentation of each step for every new drink. Mom's hidden agenda was to teach Little Joe how to neatly print. Later, she moved him into recording the creations in his drink diary in a beautiful cursive penmanship.

Edna's favorite mantra was, "People drink with their eyes. If it looks good it'll be a hit. So, create each blend with the *eye of a camera*." And he did, applying this lesson to his personal appearance and accomplishments. At the first opportunity he joined the Boy Scout system and was very successful. He loved all the organization had to offer a youngster and the motto, "Be Prepared," shaped his personality.

Through high school, he was part of the aptly named Triple Trio Rocks with whom he was allowed to carry the sheet music for the tunes, but not attempt to sing a note. Starting in ninth grade, he joined the Mind-Rockers Chess Club where he only kept track of the pieces, boards, and points because a *Sicilian Defense* was a completely different move from a *four-three defense* football strategy. As a star linebacker for the Rockers football team, Joe earned recognition and a scholarship to college.

Phoebe was looking out the windshield, mentally grinding away on the case file she would build for this investigation. She was making a concerted effort to ignore the slow ride back to the office as a passenger with the Sheriff driving. "Thanks for the ride, Joe. Don't worry about anything. I've got this covered. Enjoy your vacation and Merry Christmas to you and Mary Margaret. I suppose your girls will be home?"

"All four will be back for a few days. Undersheriff Bill will be in charge at the office, but call if you need me. If we don't talk before, Merry Christmas. Any plans?"

"I'll be at Roz's house. She's doing a Cajun dinner for a gang of us."

"Well, have fun and good luck finding out who our patient is. Keep Bill in the loop and I'll see you next year." With this final comment, Joe parked the Jeep and together they walked to the back door into the Sheriff's offices.

Noting the strong odor of burnt coffee, Joe tried not to inhale and quickened his pace past the hallway coffee pot area. It crossed his mind that someday the pot could start a fire and take out the entire building. The official 'Hallway Break Area' was a substitute for an actual break room thus saving space and discouraging frivolous chatter. The hallway had a small coffee pot nook built into the wall, no chairs, and little space for congregating. The result was shorter than average breaks and higher than average visits to the Buns coffee shop across the street from the county building. It had been contrived by a city manager whose only focus was productivity. Luckily, he eventually moved on to another unsuspecting county where he would be welcomed with open arms for the first few years.

Joe took a final look into his office to be sure everything was in order before his absence and did a quick check-in with Roz in case any last-minute details needed his attention. She saw him coming down the hallway and started a wave with her hand, "All's quiet on the western front. This is the all-clear to exit for your staycation and thanks for the big bonus!"

That comment stopped Joe halfway to his office and he reluctantly turned toward Roz, "Bonus? Oh, ha. I get it. Very funny, Roz. As they say, check's in the mail." He walked down the hallway toward the exit, quickly turning back to Roz. He smiled, nodded, gave a tug on his left ear lobe, and wished her a Merry Christmas. With that he strutted toward the back door with a vacation lift in each step, passing Phoebe who was struggling to de-layer some of her warm clothing.

One layer removed, Phoebe could see Roz sitting at the front desk and quickly stepped past the patrol room, jerking and pulling sleeves. It was quiet in the offices during the winter holidays and Phoebe could speak to Roz without raising her voice, "Hey, Roz. You did a great job coordinating Chance and his helicopter to the meeting point. The woman who was in the front seat is on her way to a Pikeview hospital, with Chance at the helm and Jon attending. She was unconscious when we last saw her."

Not looking at her, Roz continued checking her hair and makeup with a handy mirror she stored in her cosmetic drawer as Phoebe was dishing out the compliments. Keeping her eyes on the mirror to deflect the comments, she applied a dose of the Nonchalant Roz Attitude, "That's what I do, y'all. Coordinate the tough stuff and make sure our highly paid Sheriff is on track and lookin' good."

Hearing the NRA loud and clear, Phoebe chose to overlook it and added, "Got another request. Can you check out this license plate number and find the owner? I need to figure out some background on this woman who's being transported. Maybe there's some family who could be notified and called in for support. And call Billy Bob over at Green County Towing and get him pointed in the direction of the recovery location. I'm thinking you've got the coordinates."

She raised two fingers, smiled and used her nickname for Phoebe, "That's two requests, Pheb' my friend, I already put him on notice and will circle back now with the okay. I'll get right on this license plate thing. That's the fun part."

"I'm starvin'. While you're taking care of this stuff, I'll run across the street to the Buns and get a sandwich to go. Can I bring something' for ya?"

"No, thanks—already had lunch."

"OK. See you in a few. And thanks for the research."

Phoebe walked out the front door, crossed the street to the Buns and ordered a BLT. In no time the sandwich was ready and along with a coffee, she zipped back to the office in under nine minutes, a new record and on snow packed sidewalks to boot. She was anxious to get what information Roz may have found.

"It's registered to an Ellis Meredith Walker," said Roz. "Do you know who she is?"

"Yea, I know who she is. She's the person who made a crappy decision to go up the mountain on a snowy, blustery, freezing day with her dog."

"No, I mean the original Ellis Meredith. You know, the writer. And she was a politician before women could even vote."

"Ya got me, Roz. No idea. I can hardly remember what I learned in school growing up in Utah, let alone my adopted state of Colorado."

"She's not THE Ellis Meredith cuz that one died in the mid-50s. If you're a woman and you live in Colorado you know this person. Pheb', she's the Susan B. Anthony of the West who got the law passed in Colorado for women to vote. She was a great writer and that helped win over the state for women to vote. That was back in 1893. Then she went to Washington D.C. to work with THE Susan B. Anthony, her good buddy. As is said, 'the rest is history.' Who said that first?"

"I have no idea who said that but if I remember my fifth grade Utah civics class, they said Utah was the first state to pass the women's vote thing."

"Nah, Utah was doing a flip flop on women's rights. Wyoming was the first state to pass a suffrage law but it was not so much progressive as a lame attempt to get women to move west. They needed women. Probably for the obvious, usual reasons but also to get things goin' in the right direction back in 1869. Ya know?" With that comment, Roz shifted her eyebrows up with a conspiratorial smile.

She continued the summary, "Let me tell ya, Pheb' I'm not findin' much about this Walker person for your casefile, but I'll keep looking. I did find out that she works for the State 'Hysterical' Fund in Denver. I bet they love havin' an Ellis Meredith on staff."

The organization Roz was calling hysterical was the Historical Restoration Organization. The money that funded historical preservation came from legalized casino gambling in the history rich towns of Blackhawk, Cripple Creek, and Central City. Back in 1991, the only way to sell the idea of legalized gambling to the voting citizens was a mechanism to guarantee money to restore, maintain, and otherwise exploit the state's history and these towns were at the top of the list.

Winning grant money from this historical group for local projects was a convoluted process. In the end, it was usually a pittance of what was really needed. Trying to get them to part with their fund money was enough to drive grant writers mad, hence the nickname, Hysterical Fund. These good-hearted, creative, determined, and not to mention highly paid grant writers awoke to the reality of "third time's a charm." Three rounds of submitting for funds ensured continuous employment for them and abundant opportunities in salvaging Colorado history. A match made in heaven for grant writers and the towns lucky enough to tap the funds available.

The town of Oresville was trying to tap funds for major restoration of their town's main street and the history of the mining industry. First gold, then silver, and now molybdenum were the forces that created the bedrock on which Oresville was built. Roz had been lending her social skills to the efforts of acquiring grants for this long overdue cause. It was not as easy as she had expected.

Phoebe was still holding her coffee and to-go sandwich box, as she leaned against Roz's desk. "No idea what was going on back in the day. Maybe this Walker's a second cousin twice removed or something like that. Or her mother had high hopes for the daughter. Hence, the name, Ellis Meredith."

Roz was studying her computer screen and tapping keys, investigating the Meredith family, ignoring Phoebe's comment. Phoebe shoved off from Roz's desk and started back down the hallway towards the patrol room.

"Oh, hey, Pheb', I forgot to mention this. The vehicle has a Greenstone address listed. Isn't that where you went to check on Augusta's possible new hire for next spring, Hank somethin'? And then you just happen to run into this Ponytail Guy?"

Phoebe jerked to a halt, with sudden visions of Beautiful Man, Bartholomew Masterson. Several seconds passed before her breathing returned.

"Pheb', you okay? Did ya hear me?"

Phoebe hesitated and gave a quick smile, "I'm great. Just send the address over to my email. Thanks."

In a slight daze, she walked leisurely into the deserted patrol room and slowly, gently sank into a chair. A postcoital blush reddened her cheeks as she thought about the last time she saw Bart.

MAKIN' WHOOPEE

Phoebe met Beautiful Man, Bart, down in Greenstone at the end of August, a few months ago. There had been a death in Oresville and Old Al's wife lived in the city of Pikeview which was commonly called out as part of the Greater Greenstone area. There was nary a hair's breadth that separated the small town of Greenstone, population five thousand, from Pikeview, a much larger city of over 400,000. Phoebe was delivering the news of Old Al's passing to his wife, Martha, who went by the name Queennie.

The morning Phoebe arrived in Greenstone, Bart happened to be the lead patrol officer on duty, six in the morning until two in the afternoon. Their meeting was purely coincidental and carried a note of disaster. Phoebe had driven nonstop for two hours from Oresville direct to Greenstone at the butt crack of dawn, a sixteen-ounce Yeti mug at her side, and no breakfast. This was the perfect storm. One thing led to another and she passed out, dropping to the disgusting, dirty linoleum of the tight anteroom of the Greenstone Police Department. Quickly regaining consciousness, she was surrounded by the Greenstone Fire Department EMTs and looking directly into the incredibly deep blue eyes of a beautiful man who turned out to be Officer Bartholomew William Barclay Masterson, Bart to his friends.

Since then, on the pretense of checking on the kid, Hank Williams Klingfus, she called Bart for a status every ten days. Hank Williams had dropped out of Greenstone High School after his junior year and moved in a flash to the mountains to begin his life as a prospector. He landed in Oresville, living out of an old beat-up family car. There were no job offers for a seventeen-year-old drop out doing what he called an *early gap year*. Then Hank met up with Old Al.

As luck would have it, they became instant friends and Old Al had promised to teach him all about gold prospecting. Hank spent the summer learning what he could and just when he got fed up with being Old Al's Sherpa with no pay, Old Al suddenly died. Thanks to Phoebe the cause of death was determined to be arsenic poisoning, not natural causes as assumed due to his advanced age of sixty-nine.

Augusta stepped in and paid the kid with the money she harvested from Old Al's gold stash. She sent him back to Greenstone and the kid was supposed to be in high school, on track to graduate in the spring. If this actually happened, he had a job offer with Augusta back in Oresville for the coming summer, but only if he hung in there and graduated. Augusta operated her family's silver mine, The Last Hurrah, and always added summer help out of mining and engineering schools in the US. Hank would be an exception to the college prerequisite.

Phoebe took advantage of this cover and Bart seemed delighted to hear from her each time. He always had a tidbit regarding the Klingfus family and Hank's attendance in school, even though he was not a truant officer. The calls got longer with a bit of intimacy growing in their conversations. Bart called Phoebe occasionally but his timing was always off—his practice with women was limited. She was either on duty and could not talk or she was sitting with her BFFs, Roz and Carrie Jean, at the Club and would *choose* not to talk then either. His call would go to her voice mail and at the message notification beep, she would announce to their inquisitive looks, "Ponytail Guy." Carrie Jean and Roz would look at each other, then back to Phoebe, "What's goin' on here with this guy, Phoebe-girl?"

Carrie Jean reminded their little group, "Isn't this the first bit of interest since the SL-ICK relationship debacle. It's been how many years?"

"For the record, it's been way too many. But Ponytail Guy is just a professional contact with information on the high school kid who Augusta promised a job for next summer, only if he graduates. I'm keeping an eye on him for Augusta. Remember him, Hank Williams? His mom named the firstborn son after that old country western star." A smooth redirect from Phoebe who was always willing and able to steer clear of a conversation regarding men in her life or otherwise.

The last time Phoebe was in Pikeview it was the weekend after Thanksgiving. Both she and Bart had volunteered to work on the holiday to give the married officers time with their families. Phoebe announced to Ponytail Guy that she needed to get a jump on holiday shopping and she had planned a drive to the shops in Old Colorado City on Saturday, her day off. As she dressed for the one-hundred-mile drive from Oresville, she carefully selected black leggings, an ultra-low-cut tank top with a pushup bra, a down jacket, and a snazzy scarf with gold threads. Bart suggested they meet at his favorite diner for dinner before she drove back to Oresville. Mo's was a 1940's vintage diner located on the edge of Greenstone with parking and entrance in the rear.

The owners of the diner, high school friends of Bart's, Kindra and Brett, were delighted that he finally had a date. They suggested a booth at the front windows where the Christmas decorations on the main street could be seen. They happily agreed to stay open beyond the usual closing time of two in the afternoon every day of the week. This might help with the success of Bart's first date in years. With high hopes, they lowered the lights, setting the stage for this potential relationship.

Phoebe rushed into Mo's parking lot at the stroke of five sharp and saw Bart's Ram in the first parking slot. Beautiful Man was sitting in the driver's seat. She pulled next to him, and with a quick look into the rearview mirror to check her hair condition, she slid out of her Ford. Bart jumped out of his Dodge and hot-footed around the front to meet Phoebe.

"Oh Bart, the traffic was crazy out there. I was almost late!"

"Not to worry, Phoebe. I just got here myself. Hope you like this funky food joint. Friends of mine have owned it for years and they're looking forward to meeting you."

Meeting his friends now? Hmmm, that's a big step. Let's see where this takes us.

"Looks like fun. And, by the way, hi Bart. How are you?"

"Just great. And speaking of great, you look very nice tonight."

"Thanks, Bart. Please lead the way. I've worked up a great appetite with all this Christmas shopping."

Putting out his arm in a very formal way, Beautiful Man nodded at Phoebe and guided her up the steps to the door of the diner.

As they entered, Phoebe thought she had returned to the 1940's. The black and white tile floor glistened, the long soda bar with pedestal stools stood to their right and a series of booths lined the walls on the left and across the front. The lights were low and there was no one else to be seen. Bart led her to a front booth and they each slid into the cracked red leather seats, across from each other. Hanging on the wall under the large plate glass window at each booth, was an old jukebox—still functioning.

"Wow, Bart. This place is terrific. So classic. Did your friends restore it?"

"Yes, they did. Here they come now."

"Kindra, Brett, let me introduce Phoebe Korneal. Phoebe, this is Kindra and Brett.

"Nice to meet you. You've done a fantastic job with this diner. How long have you owned it?"

"We've been here several years now and love it. It seems the folks in Greenstone feel the same way and business is steady. Now, what can we serve you two tonight?"

Bart spoke up immediately. "We'll have your cheeseburgers, the works included, with extra fries to share. Two cokes on the side." Bart was not really sharp on *date procedures*. In fact, he had little practice on anything when it came to impressing women. Kindra and Brett both were standing in front of the table and while taking the order they tried not to jump in with help for Bart. He had a disappointing relationship several years ago. Nothing since. He seemed very interested in this date.

"Make mine a diet coke," chimed Phoebe.

"Oh, sorry there. I just ordered without asking you what you would like. Just out of practice on these dinner dates, I guess"

Dinner date? Oh, this is getting better by the minute. I hadn't really thought of tonight as a date, but I think I like it. Watch your step, you know what can happen when you let yourself open up.

Once the order was taken and Kindra brought the drinks, Bart and Phoebe settled in and looked at each other, each one wondering what to say next.

He is one gorgeous man, thought Phoebe. *And he seems so sincere and easy going. Could I possibly trust him? He is the first guy in a long time I would even consider as an option for a relationship. Could this be friends with benefits thing? Just take it easy and enjoy the moment, Phoebe-girl, enjoy the moment.*

"Hey, I hope cheeseburgers are okay with you. It's my go-to food group."

"Perfect. Thanks. So, how have things been going with you here in Greenstone? Busy with writing speeding tickets this holiday season?"

"The usual. Quiet in Greenstone once the tourists leave. The new chief is not keen on speeders and barking dogs. How about you?"

"The same. Worked through Thanksgiving and will work through Christmas. But I'll have New Year's off. There's always a big party at the Club on New Year's Eve. Everyone attends. Lots of fun."

"Amazingly enough, my schedule is about the same. No work on the New Year's holiday either."

"Well, if you don't already have plans for New Year's Eve, would you like to come to Oresville to enjoy the festivities? Lots of fun folks, great music, and dancing. A really good time."

"Phoebe, thanks for the invite. I accept. Just give me the time and place and I'll be there."

"You've got it."

Oh boy. Now you've done it. You and your big mouth. Now Bart will come to Oresville and the cat will be out of the bag. Roz, CJ and Augusta will be on red alert, checking out Ponytail Guy from top to bottom. And what a top to bottom there is to check out! And where will he stay? I know where I want him to stay. One step at a time, Phoebe-girl.

Dinner was great. The fries were hot and crispy and the cheeseburgers were rare, the best ever and the camaraderie between them was the special seasoning. Full to the brim, they passed on the root beer floats. Bart's two friends sensed that he was doing well and their hovering was no longer needed. Bart had a few minor relationships brought on by his local celebrity status in the sports of football and baseball. Five years ago, a serious relationship developed and when that went bust, Kindra and Brett, his best friends since middle school, became the—official surrogate relationship drones.

Bart was not born with natural talent when it came to women and the subject was usually off limits between the friends. However, Kindra operated with her radar screen ever expanding in a search for the right partner for Bart. Brett operated with a *let nature take its course attitude* and put a decisive kibosh on Kindra's finds, but not her self-appointed status as Venus, the love goddess in residence.

"Next time," grinned Bart. "We'll start with the floats."

"Great idea. I'd love that," smiled Phoebe as she thought, *Next time?*

Saying a warm goodbye to Kindra and Brett, they strolled into the moonlit parking lot. Bart was careful to have Phoebe's arm in his and she was enjoying every minute. He steered her to the passenger side.

Bart was driving a shiny, spotless, newer, black Dodge Ram 2500 truck. It was equipped with the latest gadgets, a sparkle that seemed to reflect even the dimmest of lights in the parking lot. She was thinking, *He takes good care of his truck. Check that box.*

At the invitation to continue their conversation sitting in his pickup, Phoebe had readily agreed. As Bart opened the door, she let out a loud, shocked gasp, quickly stepped back, stepping on Bart's boots. She let loose with, "Holy Shit."

"Sorry, sorry, sorry," she mumbled as she tried to stop her tilt into the door and his body. There was a surprising, intense physical energy that leaped from his chest to her shoulder and this added to the fumble. Much to Phoebe's chagrin, there were empty water bottles, sandwich wrappers, clothing, and crumpled newspapers at least two feet deep on the floor of his truck. It would be necessary to clean out a spot for her to put her feet or she could carefully step into the mass which would leave her knees propped up to her chin on top of the trash. The back seat appeared just as bad and was covered with fishing equipment, a basketball, more discarded athletic-wear, and this was noted with just a quick glance in the weak overhead light.

Quickly shoving the trash into several used sandwich bags and trying to push some of it under the front seat, he was clearing his throat with an embarrassed laugh, "Sometimes there's not a trash can around when you need one."

"Looks like you would need several cans to clear this out. Have you been collecting over the last several years or are you saving for a special event?" Phoebe was trying to modify the initial gasp into something a little less harsh. Her usual slight register on the OCD spectrum was being pressed to the limits and she recognized her love for *everything in its place and a place for everything* was spiking to major proportions. Fighting the urge to look for a shovel in an effort to help clean out the mess, she fought the temptation to say, "Step back and let me do this right."

Bart let out a little endearing giggle, "Easier than a diary and I can tell you where each of these wrappers are from and give a rating on the food quality."

Trash somewhat removed and a place for her boots to land, he helped her step into the front seat and rushed around the back end to get in, not wasting any time to get this show on the road.

Despite her reaction to his trash collection, she recognized that he had the sweetest disposition. Phoebe's mind was smiling in spite of this discombobulation.

As he settled in behind the steering wheel and started the engine, the radio suddenly came to life and blasted the song "Uptown Funk." Bart did not seem to notice and shouted over the music, "Any plans for the rest of the evening or should we go for a ride, maybe even up to my house and we can feed my pet gerbil, Marty?"

Phoebe thought she had heard something about a matey, a momma, a monkey. In an effort to clarify she yelled, "Your what?"

The music continued to blast, the subwoofer in full swing. He could see her lips move, but could not get it and quickly bent towards her, asking again. At the same time, she leaned toward him over the center console, reaching for the volume knob on the radio. She turned her face to him to be heard over the music and the sound of the heater over-working to warm the cab. They knocked heads, and his front tooth collided with her upper lip. They both fumbled for the volume control on the radio, while Phoebe tasted something metallic on her tongue.

She put her hand to her mouth and mumbled, "I think I need a napkin or something."

Bart reached under his legs to the floor and fumbled with one of the sacks of trash, desperately hoping to find an unused or slightly used napkin, "I'm so sorry. I'm so clumsy around women. It's safer to just talk on the phone."

Finding a Kleenex in her coat pocket, she pressed it to her lip, "It's okay, Bart, I just need some ice and it'll be fine."

"Say no more, I live five minutes away. We'll get your ride later." He banged the gear shift into reverse, backed out, then quickly launched into Drive. Off they went.

PLANS DIVERTED

Once they pulled into Bart's driveway, he stopped, hit the remote for the garage door. He ran around to open the passenger door for Phoebe and helped her out. The tissue she was holding was now red with blood and when she pulled it away from her lip, he could see the swelling. Her lip looked more than fat.

"Quick, let's get you into the house and put some ice on that distended lip of yours."

"Tanks lots fer cop'ment. Auch, hurt t' tak." She tried to be heard and understood.

Guiding Phoebe through the garage and up the two stairs to the kitchen entrance, he sat her down at an old,

1950's Formica table, white with multicolored speckles, and designs of little boomerangs all over it. He grabbed a paper towel and gave it to Phoebe as he reached into a cabinet for a baggie. It was quickly filled with handfuls of ice from the top freezer and he gently placed it on Phoebe's upper lip.

"Here goes, Phoebe. See if this doesn't help."

She looked at him with doubt in her eyes. Her lip felt like it had become the size of an orange and she could hardly speak audibly. The ice stung along with the disappointing pain of the direction this evening had taken.

The lip and tooth were both hurting. "Arrggg, s' bleeding. Tooth. Lip. Hurt." She was trying to not say much and still tell him it was not better with the ice.

Bart was getting chatty and added, "I'm so sorry this happened to you. We were having such a lovely, great evening, right?

She tried to indicate her agreement with just eyebrows while keeping the ice in place. With a Herculean effort to communicate by looking directly at him, she squinted her eyes and mumbled, "Thtitches."

"What? Thitches? Oh, stitches? Right, let me take a quick look at your lip. I do this lots at work. Yup, I think this will require a trip to a hospital emergency room. I happen to know the night ER nurses at one of the Pikeview hospitals."

He leveled a look directly into her eyes and tried to reassure her, "It's not really bad, but a stitch or two will help it look better down the road. Wouldn't want you looking like Frankenstein's monster from one date with me. Keep the ice on your lip and let's get to it."

Phoebe jerked at the Frankenstein comment and a horrified look that shouted, *Oh Lordy, tell me I'll not look like Cassius Clay's boxing partner the rest of my life.*

Bart ignored Phoebe's petrified look. He helped her into the passenger seat and made sure the ice was in place. He jumped in behind the wheel, backed out of the narrow, little driveway, and closed the garage door. They were off to a local hospital without the radio blaring which seemed to be what started this downhill slide into a trip to the ER.

As they drove, Phoebe thought, *Well, this didn't work out like I planned. So much for my low-cut top and the near miss kiss in the car. Geesh. Just my luck. Is this what they mean by the best laid plans of men or is it the best plans to get laid?*

Meanwhile, Bart was thinking, *Damn, I really screwed this up. We were havin' a great time, Mo's was spot on, and just when I was thinking tonight would be THE night, clumsy me. Looks like the only bed we might see tonight is the one in the ER.*

—

MORNING COCKTAIL

T wo days before Christmas, Carrie Jean and Phoebe did their usual Wednesday morning at TuTu's Washateria. Phoebe always had Wednesday off and her schedule dictated the item of laundry on Wednesday. She was trying to break the patterns in her life, but it felt so comfortable, so predictable, and besides, Wednesday was a time for these two childhood friends to hang out without interruption.

Phoebe loved to multitask, as in getting work done, socializing, having breakfast, and starting one day a week with a Bloody Mary cocktail. Hearing the town gossip as seen through the eyes of Ace Reporter, Carrie Jean, was a great break from her usual routine.

TuTu's place was the perfect confluence. Phoebe stepped through the front door into a faint cloud of early morning smells that matched the machines, complete with old soap, over-used dryer sheets, and stale appliance odor from constant use. TuTu herself was perched on a high stool at a laundry sorting table and looked to be preoccupied with stacking coins from yesterday's collection jug. Without looking up to be certain, she cheerfully called out a "Hey, Phoebe. Is it Wednesday already?" as if she were delivering opening remarks from the pulpit.

The Reverend Gabriella Trujillo Tavarez, or TuTu in the suggested colloquial, was a retired Baptist minister who was brought up in the Catholic philosophy and rituals. When someone asked her about these cultural opposites of Baptists and Catholics, she would reply, "My fire and brimstone preaching style is more Baptist-like than what's favored by the Catholic's ruling gang of honchos." Anyone hearing one of her sermons would certainly return for more. She had a natural gift for public speaking to promote, explain, and convince any audience, small or large, of her point of view. Her sermons left no doubt as to the true meaning of Christianity with organized religion's philosophies coming in at a weak second place.

After thirty years of tending her flock as a single woman of the cloth, she dropped out, and married fellow parishioner, the Retired Reverend Jorge Tavarez. Many years ago, she had been married in an impulsive romance fresh out of seminary school. An argument turned violent and she landed in a hospital for a week. Not even a month past the marriage vows, she packed her bags, moved home to New Mexico and never again spoke of the lesson learned.

Together, she and Jorge followed the sun in an old converted yellow school bus, preaching from various pulpits for vacationing ministers and practicing what they preached. Hitting burnout at year five, they landed in Oresville. For them, it was like a giant dispersed congregation with lots of potential, and living at nearly 10,500 feet was as close as one could get to heaven here on earth. TuTu and Jorge treated the townsfolk as their flock and lived the operational side of their beliefs. TuTu always lectured, "Talk is cheap, the tough part is the practice."

TuTu's Washateria promoted the motto, "Cleanliness is next to Godliness" and together they were guided by a more lenient, realistic interpretation of the Bible. Monday through Friday, Jorge served free breakfast, hot coffee, and Bloody Marys. One could never tell if there was any booze in the Mary or not. It was the thought that counted.

Always displayed was an old plastic gallon detergent jug, cut down to allow for donations as a type of collection plate. The idea of free food and drink only went so far. Anyone in need of sustenance and cleanliness would find a morning at TuTu's like a welcoming oasis in the desert. TuTu took the people in and started the machines. Jorge cooked the breakfast and served hot, heavy coffee or a Mary on request to the local insiders.

On this particular Wednesday, Carrie Jean was running late and her entrance marked a delay in the start time of their Bloodys 'n' Breakfast routine. Phoebe had ordered up a Mary to prime the pump, as TuTu noted, while the two of them were stacking coins. The washateria was quiet with only two machines in various stages of running water, spinning, gasping, and bouncing.

Carrie Jean was comin' in hot through the door announcing, "Sorry I'm late. Did ya start without me?"

Phoebe turned on the stool, leaning down to give her much shorter friend a hug in greeting, "No worries. I figured you'd get here whenever. A big, hot, news story demanding a headline?"

"Oh sure, at this hour I hope not. The truck off the road from yesterday is the only blip on the news radar today. It's always quiet for the last few weeks of the year. New Year's Eve brings out the crazy stuff that's newsworthy. What about the woman yesterday and the Flight for Life ride? Did she make it to Pikeview? Got an update for me?"

TuTu chimed in, "What's this about some woman up on Wurtz Ditch? Anyone we know?"

This is what Phoebe loved about TuTu's Washateria. The machines may be slow but the gossip was fast and furious. "Last I heard, she's alive, parked in one of the Pikeview hospitals, and Billy's towing is taking her pickup over to the garage, or it's already there. We're trying to find a significant other to notify. Roz is on it today. As of the end of my shift yesterday, nothing. I've got her name and until we find a contact, no can say. You know how that goes."

Carrie Jean chimed in. "Well, I did a little digging and that license plate is registered down in Greenstone to some guy, as single ownership. Not joint ownership like with a wife. Maybe it's the woman's dad or brother or something and she borrowed the truck. Your Ponytail Guy could be a source for this information. He lives in Greenstone, correct?"

Phoebe smiled an answer to Carrie Jean's question.

"Give me this mystery man's phone number and I'll just give him a little ringy-dingy." Carrie Jean was eager to either meet this guy or to get a scoop. The margin of difference between the two was negligible.

"CJ, someone driving off the road is not big news. Maybe a back story of poor judgement when bad weather was predicted would be more on point."

Phoebe added in a lowered voice, "He's coming up here for New Year's Eve at the Club. Maybe you can ask him in person."

C'EST BONJOUR

Carrie Jean had pulled up another stool at the sorting table and when she heard this announcement, she practically fell off it. Before she could get the details on this fresh fodder, the door suddenly swung open and Quinton bumped through it. He was hefting a heaping basket of dirty laundry, simultaneously attempting to hold open the door for Anne Louise's entrance, and balancing a to-go coffee from Becky's Buns.

Anne Louise graced the entrance with a smiling flourish. As a tall, rather stately, elderly woman, she could affect a style that was worthy of her many years on the planet. She threw a long scarf over her shoulder, patted her thick, white elaborately coiffed hair, and called out with affection in French, "Merde! (Shit)" She paused, smiling for a response.

Carrie Jean and Phoebe each reflected a bewildered look trying to interpret what she had said or perhaps closer to what she meant to say. Carrie Jean knew enough French to be dangerous and wondered if something had happened to Anne Louise as she swept through the Washateria entrance.

The French language was not within Anne Louise's skill set, even with several years immersed in the language, the country, and their Burgundy. Quinton was usually close enough to overhear the attempt to use this Romance language. He would gently, softly, and correctly repeat the intended words in English. Occasionally he would remind her of the correct word and in return he would get *the look*. She was not a person to take kindly to being corrected on anything.

He smiled and added, "She meant to say hello in French. Annie's French is on the proverbial learning curve."

With Quinton's comment, she laughed with a fake gaiety and exclaimed, "Quelle horreur (how awful)!" Uncle Q nodded to the listening group, "She meant to say, so true."

He turned to Anne Louise and said, "Darling, that would be si vrai (so true)."

"That's what I said, Dear." She gave him a steady stare using her lowered threatening voice.

Phoebe jumped into the mix with a distraction and declared, "Welcome home!" Hugs and greetings were exchanged all around and more machines were added into the noise equation.

Quinton Garrett was not Augusta's biological uncle. He was more like an affable partner to Augusta's mother, Anne Louise. He was tall, slim, silvery gray, and together he and Anne Louise made a handsome couple. He was the grounding to her vivacious style. For lack of a better term, Augusta had refashioned Quinton into Uncle Q years before he and Anne Louise had run off to live in Port-en-Bessin, France.

After traveling around Europe for months, they fell in love with the small fishing village in Normandy. It was the perfect serene location for the aging partners. Watching the fishing boats leave the harbor and motor into the English Channel always entertained them. Their biggest and only disappointment of the years in Port-en-Bessin was that Augusta never came to visit them. The excuses ran from, "The business is crazy busy right now," to, "I never leave my mountains in summer." Anne Louise gave it not a second thought and continued with her and Quinton's wonderful life on the coast of France.

Augusta was not happy to be left in charge of running the family businesses while Dear Old Mother and Uncle Q trotted off to Europe. Higgins, Inc. owned much of the main street in Oresville and additional interests in cattle, horses, silver mining, shipping, and during the 1920s,

Grandma Connie was into bootleg liquor. The family's lawyers back in Omaha, Nebraska, had directed the family's investments since the mid-1800s and the day-to-day operations were process driven without much hands-on work for Augusta. Still, she had other ideas on how to live her life that did not include taking the sole responsibility for all of the businesses. In the absence of her mother, she had her own ideas and was busy trimming, offloading, and selling whatever took too much time for too little profit.

Augusta's mother and Uncle Q's fun vacation turned into a permanent absence out of the country. What started as an adventurous train ride for a vacation across Europe on the Orient Express became a French Tourist Visa that lasted several years beyond the one-year period of expiration. When the French authorities caught up with the two elderly Americans in November, they were kindly invited to leave before the end of the year and never return.

Augusta was the only daughter of Anne Louise from an early-on short term marriage and lived in the Oresville Higgins abode during the winter season. She spent the summers roughing it in a deluxe Airstream Classic travel trailer parked high in the mountains at the family's The Last Hurrah, a silver mining operation. Augusta had a full-time manager for the mine, but its location offered an excuse for her to enjoy the short Colorado summers with camping, fishing, and hiking the mountains surrounding the Last. Augusta thought running the family businesses interfered with her chosen lifestyle and looked for every opportunity to unload those businesses that did not contribute noticeably to the bottom line.

One such line item on the yearly budget was the Higgins family homestead cabin located outside of town. When Augusta had an informal business partner, Old Al, the cabin was of little interest to her. He was called Old Al, because he was, well, old. For all intents and purposes, he was a homeless gold prospector and the lifestyle suited him. He and his faithful companion, Rose, the mule, seemed to manage fine without the accoutrements of life in the twenty first century.

For many years, Old Al lived in the Higgins cabin every winter. It was built in 1860 and the Higgins family had little use for it today. He would spend the winter fixing and repairing the cabin along with coining the gold from his summer cache. The gold from each summer of prospecting had been coined over the winter with the year it was found stamped on one side. This served to avoid banks, could be readily converted into cash as needed, and the value of each coin tracked to the gold market.

Quinton was a retired assayer in the Arkansas Valley. Before he and Anne Louise left for Europe many years ago, Quinton had taught Old Al how to operate the equipment built by Great Grandpa Higgins. Processing the gold into coins each winter and stashing it under the floor at the Higgins cabin was easier than having Rose carry it through the mountains all summer. His gold was safely hidden at the cabin until he unexpectedly passed away last

August. Now the gold coins from previous years and the nuggets from the current summer were in jars stashed in Augusta's kitchen in Oresville.

With the passing of Old Al, the work of maintaining the cabin fell to Augusta. She came to the realization that without her mother and Uncle Q to help with the attention it deserved, all would fall on her. This was the last straw and Augusta took it upon herself to unload the anticipated burden of the cabin.

Over-thinking what to do with the family homestead, last August she had taken the bold step of setting it on fire with the intention of converting the entire sections of land to a Colorado Conservation Easement. She was banking on the response time of the all-volunteer Oresville fire department, which would include thirty minutes for the volunteers to get to the firehouse, suit up, and then another forty minutes or so to get to the cabin. In her haste to be on time to Old Al's memorial service, she had ripped up the floorboards to expose the jars of gold coins. She loaded these jars into a backpack and, as she stepped out of the cabin, dropped a match to the gasoline she had emptied on the floor. Smiling to herself, Augusta drove her two passenger all-terrain vehicle down the mountain, arriving at Old Al's memorial service in time to buy a round of cocktails with her friends before the service.

She felt much better with one less thing to worry about and her mother, Anne Louise, would not be happy. So there.

Amazingly enough, the cabin did not burn to the ground. The one hundred and fifty-year old logs of the cabin were badly scorched, the roof was gone, and the floor was missing here and there. The rock fireplace was still standing, mostly, and the remains gradually would return to the earth. When the annual November turkey shoot fundraiser came up for the fire department, she contributed handsomely.

HUNGER PLANS

The talk throughout the Wednesday laundry process of snapping, folding, and hanging was all about the coming holiday. The B.P.O.E. Club always featured a Christmas Eve gathering starting at four in the afternoon and ending in time for family festivities. It was great fun for the participants and a dry run for the New Year's Eve party.

The past Elks Exalted Ruler and club manager, Willie Friedrich, and his longtime partner, Rose Mary, commandeered a few local teenagers. Elf attire had been accumulated over the past thirty years and the teenagers dressed in the faded green costumes. They worked to string up blinking colored lights around the hall and secured the giant Christmas tree for the community's kids to decorate.

Free appetizers, a community potluck, and traditional oyster stew accompanied Sheriff Joe's holiday libation chosen from his famous drink diary. A collection was always taken for the local food bank and Augusta matched dollar for dollar what was collected. In spite of the rough attitude she carried, her Higgins Family generosity continued.

The visit from Santa happened at five thirty sharp. This was meant to cover all age groups regardless of Santa beliefs. Every kid in town, if pre-registered, got a special big gift. Surprise gifts for that special someone were encouraged. Santa and his helper delighted in shouting out the name as an unsuspecting surprised adult would get a shocked look, place a hand to the heart as if the Big One were hitting, and stumble over to the seated Santa for the unexpected gift.

It was great fun to be on the observation side of this event. Those gathered at the bar shared meaningful glances and predictions of who would be embarrassed next. All were in good spirits, enjoying the festive atmosphere created by Willie, Rose Mary, and their crew of elves.

The planning at TuTu's Washateria was no different this year. They were busy debating what to contribute to the Christmas Eve heavy appetizer assortment and what would be brought in for the unexpected, surprise gifts for some of the adults. The surprise gifts were always fun and the recipients were usually caught off guard and occasionally embarrassed.

At the top of the conversation list was the continuing discussion as to the consequences of driving in a snowstorm on a forest service road up in the mountains. Carrie Jean was promoting the suggestion of calling the Ponytail Guy in Greenstone to get the lowdown on the person who was the registered owner on this truck. "Come on, Phoebe, just one little ole call to this guy will probably tell us about the vic' lying in the hospital and get you a family name for an 'occurrence with injuries' notification. Just think about it. No harm, no foul." She was in rare whining mode this morning.

Phoebe had known her buddy CJ, short for Carrie Jean, for a long time and knew better than to be persuaded into doing a rush job on this identification. The idea to call Bart, the Ponytail Guy, was a solid one, but not sitting in TuTu's Washateria on a Wednesday morning, her day off. Who knows what he would say, causing her to evoke a non-stop smile and maybe even blush. Just hearing his soft, strong voice sent a longing through her body.

Their last face to face meeting had ended in disaster. She spent the night at his place in his bed, oh yes, but with stitches in her top lip and an ice bag to keep the swelling down. He slept on the couch and checked on her welfare every two hours.

Her intended plans for an exciting night of stimulating conversation ending in rollicking sex instead became a less than lovely visit to a local hospital in Pikeview. The nurses all knew Bart by first name and

119

conducted unconscionable flirting. For several years, he was the coach for the Bedpan Bedlam ladies' softball team. Most of the nurses worked nights at the hospital, giving them the daytime to play ball. Spending quite a bit of time with them, Bart was immune to their flirting and was glad for the attention he was bringing to Phoebe.

Since then, they had talked on the phone every other day or so. He worked an opposite shift that was the busiest of the day—the morning shift. She worked an evening shift that made conversations short at best. When they did talk for longer than five or ten minutes, it was wonderful and the stress was mounting for his anticipated visit to Oresville for the New Year's Eve party at the Club.

Phoebe was thinking she would call him as soon as she got back to the rented trailer on the pretext of official business.

Anne Louise and Quinton finished breakfast, cocktails, laundry, and drifted out the door. She waved to the women in the Washateria and called over her shoulder, "Bonjour (hello) everyone. See you for Christmas dessert on Friday night."

Uncle Q chuckled looking to the ladies sitting at the counter. "She meant au revoir (goodbye), right, my dear?"

Anne Louise was nearly out the door when she stopped to fix an unhappy smile on him with a frosty look, "Whatever, Dear."

TuTu was curious about the victim and the comment around the report dead or worse. If the person was local, why would she be up on a mountain trail in a storm?

While Carrie Jean was wrestling clothes between machines, TuTu quickly turned to Phoebe and with a lowered voice, asked for the name of the woman. "You know I run a monthly seminar for people wanting to heal their toxic relationships. We do weekly calls plus each month an in-person gathering here in town. We had one this last weekend and I'm worried this woman may have been with us. It was over on Sunday and this happened yesterday, Tuesday?"

Phoebe deliberately folded her arms into a relaxed stance and dropped into the back of the stool, "No, we're not clear when it happened. She was found yesterday and it looked like she had been there through the storm or part of it anyway."

"But she's alive, right?"

"Right, but for now I can't help you. Once I get her family or a significant other notified, I can give you a call. Info is slow comin' in during the holidays so it could be tomorrow. I'm off today. Will that work?"

TuTu rested her elbows on the table, folded her hands as if in prayer, and reluctantly agreed, "I guess it'll have to do. Did someone say there's a dog in the formula here? What happened to it?"

"Yup. The dog is currently over at Augusta's house. She still has Old Al's mule, Rose, too and that's not going well. It's an old, ornery cuss and scares the neighbors, chases off the postman, and bays at the moon. He probably doesn't care much for living in Oresville's suburbia." They had to laugh at the image this conjured up.

Phoebe thought it was strange that TuTu would ask about a dog. Also, TuTu named Wurtz Ditch and neither the dog nor the Ditch was mentioned in all the talk this morning. Probably the town's gossip circuit again.

After taking her clean clothes to the car, Carrie Jean returned to talk with Phoebe and TuTu. Their conversations drifted to the possibilities of Roz's Cajun dinner menu and what they could bring for the assigned cocktails and appetizers. It would be an intimate gathering of friends for the holiday dinner. Roz had included not only Phoebe and Carrie Jean, but also Bill Diamond, and Carrie Jean's latest squeeze, Brian, the bartender from the Club. She had an old friend, Laurie Watson, from her early years working in Pikeview when she moved to Colorado after high school. Laurie was the niece of Doc Watson, the Green County Coroner. He and Laurie would be joining them, too.

TuTu and Jorge were planning to enjoy Christmas dinner at Augusta's house, prepared by newcomer, Queennie, Old Al's widow. Queennie was a resident of Pikeview where she owned an automobile repair shop but enjoyed the high country and her newly forged friendship with Augusta. Plus, she loved to cook and was in charge of the holiday meal for Augusta, Anne Louise, Quinton, TuTu, and Jorge. The plan was the group at Roz's house would travel over to Augusta's for a little celebration and dessert later Christmas evening.

Roz was a great cook as long as she stayed away from potato salad. She had only one blemish on her culinary track record and that was a dish at the memorial service and community potluck for Old Al. Roz had organized the buffet and recruited her friend, Libby, to help. The salad was interesting because the potatoes were unusually crunchy to the point of tooth splitting hard. Roz was hoping the townsfolk would forget this transgression and she could retain her reputation for putting the "P" in Party.

As usual, the morning flew by and Carrie Jean needed to get back to work. Under the guise of needing to get home to do more of the daily clean, Phoebe was keen to get back to her trailer. Her mail-order black satin chemise should be arriving any day, and she couldn't wait to see it. Maybe she could try it on and call Bart at the same time. This would be practice for wearing something other than worn out, frayed, sweats to sleep in.

She parked beside the rented trailer and the package was already at the door. She picked it up, balanced her handbag, the laundry basket and supplies, pushed through the door into the kitchen, and abruptly dropped everything on the counter. The package was the priority and everything else could wait.

It was discreetly wrapped in plain paper and took a bit of effort to open with a kitchen knife. Phoebe immediately walked down the hallway, clothing stripped on the way, shoes left in her wake. She was excited to try on this "first of its kind" purchase. Living in the mountains, a clean, pressed pair of jeans and low-cut top under a jacket or denim shirt was plenty for this lifestyle all year long. Phoebe slipped the silky garment on and it fit perfectly. *Wow, is this me lookin' hot? Yeah! New Year's Eve, bring it on!*

BEAUTIFUL MAN

Phoebe was still wearing the new negligee as she called Bart, using a work-related question as an excuse to talk to him. Although she was feeling good about herself, there was some anxiety about their upcoming date for the party at the Club followed by his first overnight visit at her rented trailer.

After the disastrous ending to her visit following Thanksgiving, they had not seen each other. Phoebe had a faint redness on her lip from that dinner date. She wondered what this visit would bring. *Why do I get so jittery when I think about talking to Bart? Just settle down. After all, this is just a business call, isn't it? He's the first guy in years that has interested me. The SL-ICK relationship collapse was devastating and I don't want to do that again. Do I dare take this relationship further? Is he up for something beyond casual? Let nature take its course and maybe just enjoy the ride, right?*

"Hey, Phoebe. How's it goin'?" He didn't hesitate one second to respond to her call. *When she calls it makes my day.*

"Good, Bart. And how are you doin'?"

"No complaints. Just on a break this morning, nothing much is happening. Gotta love it."

"Today's my day off, but I do have a work question."

I hope it's not the only reason she called me, Beautiful Man mused. *Seems like each time I hear her voice I want to stay on the phone for hours, and likely a phone call will not create a trip to the ER.* "Anything I can do to help, I hope you know."

"Remember I told you about the woman who was found off the road, up in my neck of the woods? The call came in as dead or worse."

They both laughed at this reminder. How people call in to describe an event or a crime is always a comfortable way to take out the constant stress around law enforcement. Roz always said she would write a book someday about the calls she has taken for the Green County Sheriff.

"Well, anyway, now she's in a hospital over by you in Pikeview. Any chance you might know who she is? Her name is Ellis Walker and she might be from your town, Greenstone. She was in a vehicle registered there to a Michael Walker. Might be a husband, brother, something."

"You're kidding me. Ellis Meredith Walker?" Bart's voice went up at least a full octave in disbelief. "I know her and I know about her. Wonder what she was doin' up in your county?"

"Well, that's what we'd like to find out. Why would she be up on a mountain, over one hundred miles from her home, when a big snow storm was predicted? Can you share what you know about her?"

"You bet I can, Phoebe. I had a domestic call to her home not too long ago and that was not the first one."

"What kind of a domestic? A domestic can mean all kinds of different things. Is it a case of an abusive husband? I've had those calls before but more often back in Utah than here."

Bart waited a half-beat before answering. "Well, no. Actually, it's the other way around."

"Her husband called for help?"

"No. According to the neighbors, it sounded like all hell was breaking loose in the Walker house again, and they made the call, not hubby."

Phoebe was silent, taking this in. This was a new scenario for her. The guy being abused is not common or commonly reported. The usual statistic is that one in nine men experience some form of domestic abuse while the rate for women is much more frequent, at one in four. And the

129

stats in Colorado for men under the age of fifty are only fifteen percent of the total. Not much for younger guys.

Bart continued with the details, "Seems she was getting a bit aggressive, like throwing plates and glasses at him. At the rate she was going, the only thing left to throw would have been the kitchen knives. The place was trashed. There were broken shards of not exactly Swarovski Crystal everywhere. Chunks of dinner plates covered the floor. They must be using paper plates and red plastic cups now." He had to chuckle at this possibility.

"No wonder the neighbors called for help. What's the husband's name?"

"Michael Walker. And of course, he refused to press charges after everything quieted down. This is the second or third time in the last year. They've only been married a few years and just moved to Greenstone a year or so ago. They're definitely young." Phoebe was listening closely to every word, trying to add her own prejudice as context.

"Nice guy, helped everyone in the neighborhood. He's rather meek and mild, and was visibly shaken when my partner and I arrived. Ellis, on the other hand, was certainly agitated. We were able to separate them and when I spoke with her, she calmed down. Her side was that she was afraid of her husband and was just trying to protect herself. I didn't buy it, but the husband decided not to press charges, so there was nothing we could do. I warned her to keep things under control and think twice about the noise level for the neighborhood. She said she would, and promised all would be quiet going forward."

"Did that stick? Did you get any more calls to their place?"

"No, none. While I was talking with Ellis, my partner was talking with Michael and he appeared to be embarrassed yet relieved that we had arrived to de-escalate whatever was going on between the two of them. He related that she has a serious anger management problem. Whenever he did not agree with her, she would lose her temper, at times worse than others. That evening was definitely one of the worst. It would take them or her or him all night to clean up the mess. He shared with us that he could see her anger escalating even though she attends a therapy weekend once a month and regular support calls. We could tell he was worried."

"Michael Walker? Hum, I probably need to notify him that she's in the hospital from this wreck."

"He might not care much. Shortly after 'the event,' he filed a restraining order against her and left town."

"Where'd he go?"

"You're not going to believe this, Phoebe, I heard he went to Oresville."

Mentally Phoebe weighed these morsels. Michael Walker. Michael Walker. "Does he use a nickname?"

"Yup. Everyone called him Mickey."

"What?" Phoebe practically choked on the word. "We have a Mickey Walker working at our office. A new hire, working as a janitor and general handyman. A young guy. Could he be the one and same?"

"Tell you what, Phoebe, when I get a spare minute or ten on duty today I'll check out their house down here. See what I can find. I'll give you a call this evening and fill you in. How's that?"

"Great, Bart. Thanks a lot for the help. And, it was good to hear your voice." *If you only knew how good.* Again, a longing went through her. One that had been buried for years.

"You too. Catch ya later as soon as I have some info." He could hear her warm smile. *Even if I have to make something up. Just so I can hear your voice again.*

HOT ON THE TRAIL

Phoebe called the office to talk with Roz, who was busy doing a light touch-up on her makeup. She fumbled the headset into place, and announced, "Good afternoon. Green County Sheriff's Office. Rosalind Marie Beaudreau speaking."

"Roz, it's me, Phoebe."

"Y'all interrupted my make-up session. It's wonderful being here when it's so quiet. I can do make-up, touch up the nails, try a new hair style, and no one knows for the better." Roz was tickled that business was slow. She could tend to her holiday persona and plans for the Cajun dinner she was hosting.

"Sorry about that. I've a quick question for you. Have ya seen the new guy, Mickey Walker, today?"

"I'm thinking this is your day off. Why ya checking out this guy? I think he's too young for us. Wait. Do you know somethin' I don't know?"

"Since when has 'too young' become part of your vocabulary, Sista?"

"Key point. With a scarcity of eligible possibilities, I might be changin' up my standards," laughed Roz.

"Too many questions. And yes, this is my day off and yes, he's likely too young for us. I think it's a coincidence that he's Mickey Walker and the 'maybe dead or worse' driver off the road yesterday is Ellis Walker. Right? You know what I always say about coincidence?"

"No such thing. I seem to remember hearin' that from you a time or two. I'll do some work on my end today, it's quiet in the office, seeing if I can find a connection between those two. When and if I find something, I'll give you a call. I take off at noon tomorrow to decorate for the Christmas Eve event at the Club, ya know. I'd like it to look *over the top* for the kiddos. You'll be able to give me some help on this, I hope?"

"Of course, don't I help you every year? It's always fun to light it up, then watch the teenagers come draggin' in with parents when they could be home playing video games. They get in the door and, like, wow, let the party begin." Phoebe was laughing about the vision of teens being dragged into the Club and the change once they got there.

"It's fun for sure. Then the work's over until New Year's Eve. The place looks nice for the week, and sparkly for the party. Y'all gotta be prepared for the end of the year bash. It's the two birds with one stone thing, ya know."

Phoebe nodded in agreement, "Yup, I get it. I'm probably goin' too far regarding someone stuck in a storm, but we need to understand who she is and why she was on the mountain, in a truck that isn't hers. Credit card records could give us an idea as to where she stayed up here, if she didn't do a same day round trip from Greenstone to Oresville and back."

"That's a possibility, especially if she didn't have a suitcase or some clothes for an overnight stay, ya know. She works at the hysterical society, and we're trying to get grants for the downtown restoration. Maybe she was here to sneak around and look at Oresville without anyone knowin'. They do that, ya know."

"Sneaking around? That'd be weird. Why?"

"Oh, just to get a feel for the place. I'm part of the group helpin' on the grant, but a ton of pictures went with it. We tried to show how badly in need of help we are." Roz's thinking was stuck on the grant request and the photos were necessary if they were to win the award.

"Well, whatever. Back to this real work request. I'd like to check out the new guy. Would you please check Mickey's schedule, and see if he's in the building? If he's there, I'm comin' in to have a little talk with this guy right now, day off or not."

"Sure. Hold a minute." Roz checked the schedule. Mickey was in fact supposed to be working.

She called the county front desk, "Hey Suzanne, have you seen the new guy, Mickey Walker, today? I know he's scheduled, but is he around?"

"Yes Ma'am, as a matter of fact he's standing right here. We're havin' a little chat." She let out a flirtatious giggle.

Roz wondered what in the world was up with the giggle, and decided to get the lowdown on that later. "Great. Would you send him over to my office?" Roz assumed ownership for the entire Green County Sheriff's offices. It was just easier to suggest the office was hers. She could cut through the red tape faster than if she were merely the receptionist for the department.

"Will do, Rosalind Marie Beaudreau." She ended the call with another teasing giggle.

Roz punched the phone button to pick up Phoebe holding on the other line. The Sheriff was never one to rush into any new-fangled technology. He fought tooth and nail any ideas that involved digital this, keyless that, and the fancy ideas that accompanied technology upgrades, enhancements, or integrations. Accordingly, the offices still had six buttons, black telephone sets on every desk with the one addition at Roz's desk. Hers was the standard six button keyset side by side with the latest emergency reporting equipment.

The old phone on Roz's desk also accessed the interoffice paging system dating to the 80s. Something was wrong with it. Whenever she paged someone, or made an announcement, it was set permanently at a number ten for volume control, and her voice boomed throughout the spaces. The casual visitor would instinctively duck as if there were incoming projectiles of some sort.

Volume control was just one of the many problems with the phone system. There was no one left who could fix this equipment. It was custom designed, produced, and installed before the technicians today were born. The County Administrator who had it set up was long gone. He was the same administrator who designed the Refreshment Station Hallway in the Sheriff's offices to better utilize space, speed up productivity, and get people standing as a form of exercise during coffee breaks.

Roz pushed the button to access the line where Phoebe was holding, "Hey, I'm back. Suzanne's sending him over as we speak."

"Great, Roz. Have him sit in the conference room. Offer some coffee or somethin' till I can get there in about twenty-six minutes. And thanks." Phoebe pulled off the negligee, tossed it on a chair, threw herself onto the bed to wiggle into the tight, off-duty jeans, redid this morning's ponytail, donned a black turtleneck sweater, and pinned the deputy badge to it. She suddenly had a newfound energy for doing a little unofficial detecting on her day off. She was out the door in a flash.

UNCONSTRAINED COMMOTION

The conference room was the first door in the hallway leading from the entrance off the building's parking lot. Phoebe glanced at her watch as she entered the conference room. She arrived at the twenty-five-minute mark, and could not repress a smile. *On time again. Gotta love it.* Pleased with the impeccable timing, she had to remind herself to stop obsessing about being on time down to the minute. *Relax a bit Phoebe. It's good for your health.*

Mickey had on jeans, work boots, and a county issued dark green shirt with his name badge over the front pocket. His winter jacket was draped on the back of his chair. She had only seen him working outside wearing a heavy overcoat on snow removal duty. For some strange reason, Phoebe had a quick thought that Mickey looked more like a young Doc Holliday, scrawny and weak. Holliday's self-built reputation was created around tough guy stuff in the 1800s—gun duels, knife fights, and the frivolous comment, "This is funny" when he was on his deathbed. He also requested a shot of whiskey, but Mickey did not look the type for this kind of behavior.

He resembled Holliday only in height. Phoebe expected without the heavy overcoat, he would be muscular and strong looking—like a tough guy. She was momentarily surprised by her prejudice as that wasn't the case. Mickey was average size, and not particularly buff. She had assumed that in an abusive relationship, the abusers were big, tough men. She had it directly from Ponytail Guy, it was the other way around in this instance. A big tough female. Nope, that did not fit what she had seen on the rescue mission yesterday. A paradigm shift was needed here.

Mickey was fidgeting with his cell phone. The giant coffee Roz gave him was untouched, and pushed to the side. His hair was spiked in the style favored by those under a certain age, but was not dyed a bright color. Shocking hair color was not forbidden for Green County employees, but not encouraged either. His spiky blond hair acted like an arrow pointing to his remarkable green eyes.

Phoebe was trying to look friendly as she took the chair at the end of the table next to him, "Hey, Mickey."

He glanced over to her with a low, pleasant-sounding voice, "Hello, Deputy Korneal."

"Actually, it's pronounced Cor-Nell, but you can call me Phoebe. After all, we're on the same payroll, right?" She chuckled at this little sidebar humor and continued, "So how's the new job going?"

"It's goin' okay. I'm learnin' the ropes. People are real nice to me."

Mickey quickly glanced at the back of Phoebe's chair, not directly at her, and then out the window to the main street of Oresville. He was opening and closing his flip phone on the table with one hand while the other was a white-knuckle grip on the arm of the conference room chair.

Just then Bill Diamond leaned into the conference room. Bill was the Green County Undersheriff, and in the absence of the vacationing Sheriff Joe, he was in charge. He had a surprised look to see Phoebe on her day off, and was thinking, *uh oh, overtime. Never a good thing.*

"Oh. Hi there. I was just going to turn off the lights in here. We want to manage the County's electric bill, ya know." With that said, he paused with his self-proclaimed million-dollar smile, looking for concurrence from one of them.

Hearing nothing by way of explanation he added, "What's up, Deputy Korneal?"

"Just having a chat with one of our newest employees, Mickey here."

"Well, okay, but we need to keep an eye on our overtime, don't ya know."

"Ah, sure. No problem. I'm on my own time here, so no worries."

Diamond decided this was not enough explanation, and invited himself into the room. He strolled over to a chair on the other side of the interviewee. Mickey took on a look of pure panic and confusion as his head swiveled from Phoebe, over to Bill, and back to Phoebe. He then scooted his chair away from the table, and concentrated on his cell phone. He flipped the lid open and then snapped it closed with a click—open, click, open, click.

Bill was smiling, all friendly-like, and offered his hand to Mickey for an introductory shake, "I'm the Acting Green County Sheriff, Officer Diamond. I haven't had a chance to welcome you to our little team of county employees. Mind if I sit in?"

Phoebe cringed at the thought of his comment "Acting Sheriff," and wondered what happened to the undersheriff title. Maybe there was an opening coming up in the office? She was surprised he hadn't added "O Great Benevolent Leader" to his title. A pained expression crossed her face. She could hear her half-assed plan starting to fall apart in tinkling little pieces.

With a quick nod as acknowledgement, she ignored his intrusion. Plowing forward with the interview, cleared her throat, and continued where she had left off, "Mickey, I wanted to circle back to yesterday when Sheriff Joe was talking with you. When he and I were leaving the parking lot, you looked like you had something to say. But we were in a hurry, if you remember?"

Now he was concentrating on his cell phone and flipping the cover open and closed faster. Phoebe noticed this and wondered if this could be a *tell* as to his involvement.

"No, I didn't have anything to say. Just finishing the parking lot, like the sheriff wanted. Whoever did this before I was here, didn't do a very good job. What little snow we've gotten so far is packed down, and we have four or five more months of winter comin'."

Diamond interrupted, "Hey Phoebe, were you two responding to the truck off the road with the dead body or worse?"

Hearing this, Mickey stopped snapping the flip phone's cover. He started to jiggle his foot up and down like there was some jive music going on in his brain. This time he actually looked directly at Phoebe, wondering where this conversation was going. He swiveled his body to Bill with a wide-eyed look as if to affirm his presence, adding a mind meld of "get me outta here."

Bill's face was frozen with his wide, friendly smile.

Phoebe gave a slight nod to Bill, and went on, "So you recently moved up here, is that right? Where'd you move from?" *Careful, Phoebe, just one question at a time. Interviewing 101.*

"Greenstone, next door to Pikeview."

"Did your wife come with you?"

Mickey went into a loud coughing fit at this comment, and tried to grab some of the cold coffee. He was

145

shaking his head; his eyes were starting to stream. He dropped the large coffee on the trip to his mouth. It shot out of the cup as if free of gravity. Phoebe and Bill watched it fly. The coughing worsened, and Phoebe was wondering if a Heimlich procedure would be needed.

Without another thought, she jumped up, stepped to Mickey's side, and started pounding on his back. Bill Diamond quickly stood but not fast enough. The entire large cup of coffee had assumed the shape of a wide arc. The ocean of brown, sugared liquid was on a flight path his way.

Hearing the commotion, Roz jumped up from her desk, and appeared at the conference room doorway with a questioning look in her eyes.

"Everyone okay in here?" No answer was forthcoming.

She spotted the coffee mess, and went into double time, hurried over to a cabinet, and pulled out a roll of toilet paper. This was an unlikely spot for storing bathroom supplies, but she seemed unfazed. "Well, y'all? Is everything okay?" she yelled over the coughing, the pounding, and Bill's muttered cuss words. Mopping up the mess from the large cup of coffee with toilet paper was not working. It was tissue, not paper towels. She gave up, and began multi-tasking. Armed with a wad of toilet tissue in each hand, a delighted gleam in her eye, she tried to rub the liquid from the front of the Undersheriff's pants with her right hand, and blot Mickey's shirt with her other hand.

"Yeah, Roz. Just a friendly little chat that went down the wrong pipe. Right, Mickey?" Phoebe continued hammering on his back to clear the whatever. The action on his back served only to exacerbate the coughing, the hacking, the choking.

Diamond elbowed Roz aside, grabbed more toilet paper, and declared, "I've got it. No need for any of that kind of help, Sweetie."

Hearing this, Roz's face grew into a blush. She upped her attention over to Mickey as she feigned a motherly instinct, pulled more tissue from the roll, and tried to wipe Mickey's nose to console him. "There, there. We're not trying to kill off anyone with our coffee. Wanna refresh?"

Now the toilet paper was leaving a trail of brown flakes and flotsam as the remaining amount of coffee spread horizontally along the edge of the conference table, looking for another unsuspecting human sponge. Roz put the toilet roll on the side most likely to continue to spread, and gave the Undersheriff an embarrassed yet meaningful glance.

Phoebe picked up on this, and wondered if she was becoming delusional, thinking, *What's this? Are these two trading a moment?*

Just then, Carrie Jean appeared at the door, took in the setting, and her mouth dropped open. She found the right words for the spectacle, "This is looking' like the bar scene from an early Star Wars movie."

They stopped what they were doing. The room went silent as they looked at her. This one sentence cut to the chase, and stress drained from the room. Carrie Jean invited herself in, and looked for a dry chair to sit in. The rest of them moved to the other end of the table. Bill, Phoebe, Roz, and Mickey pulled out clean, dry chairs to sit in. Each had a look of anticipation on their face, looking at the trail of toilet paper spread over the table, and Bill Diamond's crotch. Carrie Jean did not ask for details.

Mickey had a bright red, blotchy color over most of his pale skin. He was clearly embarrassed with these two women trying to help him or kill him. The new hire had a dab of TP poking out of one nostril.

The coughing and gagging subsided. He started fanning his face with both hands, and his voice came out as a high-pitched, strained falsetto, "No, I mean it's yes. It's okay. And no, my wife didn't come with me."

Roz and Phoebe traded knowing looks over this comment. Roz softly asked, "Ahhh, alrighty then. So, what's your wife's name?"

"Ellis Walker."

Roz took a breath to continue. Phoebe quickly raised a hand with a finger pointing up attempting to quiet Roz, and jumped in with a loud, accusatory voice, "Did you know that she was found yesterday stuck in a pickup off a mountain track? Left for dead, or maybe worse?"

Then Carrie Jean cleared her throat and began to say something, but before she could speak Mickey blurted,

"No, I didn't know. Where?" He did not appear to be surprised or shocked, and continued to occupy himself by wiping his eyes, dabbing coffee from his shirtsleeve, clearing his throat, and otherwise acting distracted while the dab of TP fluttered from his nose.

Phoebe ignored his question. Everyone at the table looked at him for an added comment. There followed the silence of a New York Minute, and she lowered her voice to a practiced, professional, hard, flatline level, "Did you see her? Was she up here with you over the weekend?"

"No, no, I haven't seen or heard from her in a long time. We're separated, kind of. She works in Denver and commutes from Greenstone."

"You're sure you haven't seen or heard from her in a while?"

Mickey shook his head no.

"For real? I can do some checking, ya know."

"No, I'm sure. Besides, I work Sunday through Wednesday and she works the weekdays. We're on different schedules. No chance I'll be seeing her anytime soon. I hope."

Phoebe deliberately leaned back in her chair, narrowed her eyes with an "I mean business" stare to scare even an innocent person into a confession. The conspicuous quiet was busted when the front office phone started to ring. Roz let out a little yip and raced out of the conference room.

Phoebe had been holding her breath and let out a burst of air, "Was your wife doing any kind of relationship therapy sessions, do you know?"

Mickey was blinking his eyes, cleared his throat, and croaked, "Nope."

Those remaining at the table stared at him. They wondered what he would say next. Carrie Jean was leaning forward over the table, and appeared to be holding her breath in baited anticipation. Mickey finally looked at Phoebe, took a deep sigh, and asked "What about my dog?"

Before she could think twice about continuing the interview, she pressed her lips together then answered, "Your Fido is over at Augusta Ledbetter's house. Ya know where the old Higgins property is on the edge of town? That's Augusta's house."

He looked down at his cell phone and mumbled, "I guess I should go get my dog. It's quittin' time."

Knowing what she had picked up from Bart, Phoebe looked at him with a sudden bit of sympathy. "You do that. But I'm thinking if your wife is in a hospital in Pikeview, kind of separated or not, you should haul your butt on down there, and take care of her. Ya get my drift?"

Mickey looked at her like she was utterly clueless. Without another word, he stood up to leave the room. He looked drained like a whipped pup, pulled his jacket from the back of a chair, and carefully stepped from the room.

Phoebe looked at Carrie Jean and Bill, pulled out the cell phone from her jacket pocket, and hit the stop button. "Well, there you have it. Deny. Deny. Deny." She had turned on her phone's recorder at the start of this unofficial conversation and was thinking, *How did he know the dog was up here?*

This unofficial interview didn't yield the information she had hoped to get. Things just weren't adding up. Phoebe, Bill, and Carrie Jean, turned in unison to the front window of the conference room and watched Mickey depart the county building. He walked up Main Street.

Bill wanted to know what Phoebe was up to on her day off investigating an accident. This interview or conversation or whatever it was, did not yield any useful information. This case was just another unfortunate occurrence. No overtime would be needed for something like this, yet here she was.

Carrie Jean was thinking about tomorrow's banner for her E-Blast! and she was seeing a blank spot where some juicy news should be.

Feeling frustrated and sounding it too, Phoebe huffed, "Look, I wanted to talk with him to see if he had anything for us on the thing up on Wurtz Ditch. Turns out he's separated from his wife. We're back to square one." She looked at Carrie Jean and dropped her shoulders, "No big news story for you on this one. Sorry, CJ." She purposely did not bring up the damn dog. It felt like between TuTu and Mickey, the dog had something more to do with this situation than meets the eye, and neither one of them was giving up all they knew.

The Acting Sheriff had heard enough, and took off for the men's room in an attempt to save his pants. Carrie Jean remained in her chair at the table, wondering what had transpired here. She had seen this dog yesterday at the rescue, but is it the husband's? She decided to catch up to this Mickey character. Maybe buy him a coffee at the Buns. With that thought, she bid Phoebe a quick adieu, and did a fast walk out of the conference room. She had more questions than answers.

Phoebe went up front, thanked Roz, and on the ride home she reviewed the information, precious little as it was. She knew Ellis was the person stranded on the mountain with a dog. Mickey swore he didn't know about the accident, but he knew enough to ask about his dog. Bart had said Mickey and Ellis had a rocky marriage, with Ellis being the aggressor. And Mickey said he hadn't seen her in a long time. *Hmmm, how did Ellis get hubby's dog with her outside of Oresville in a snowstorm? Two and two aren't adding up.*

Phoebe entered the front door of her rented trailer. The landline phone was ringing. She grabbed at it just as the answering machine picked up.

"Carpe diem," she yelled into the receiver. She thought *carpe diem* in place of *seize the day* was more sophisticated than "I'm having a great day and you should have one too." She was using that for the last week or two and by last Saturday it had failed the taste test. This week's greeting was all about her new priority on a daily life with less stress, more flexibility, and getting a new *Phoebe Life*. Always smart to start small and build from there. She looked to the heavens and muttered thanks to her Grandma Caroline for this lesson every time she answered her private line. However, this late afternoon she was thinking, *For this day, carpe diem is more like a balloon with a slow leak.*

"Hey, Phoebe, Bart here."

Spirits instantly lifted, she smiled, "Hi. Hey, give me a sec. I just walked in the door."

Phoebe pushed the stop button on the ancient answering machine, quickly shed jacket, hat, and gloves to the floor, settled into a kitchen chair, and let out a sigh of relief, "There, that's better. Got something good to tell me, Sweetie?" She was shocked at this Freudian slip. *Did I overstep the bounds between us? OMG, what have I done?*

She heard a low, awkward laugh coming over the telephone line, but he did not comment. Bart was delighted at hearing this term but he mentally fumbled a reaction to it. He was not comfortable at all when it came to something more than a neutral, friendly conversation with women.

"What's the carpe diem all about? A special food, a greeting in French, what?"

"Just trying to get a jump on my life. I'm trying to take the 'work, clean, repeat' thing to another level, like have some fun, ya know?"

"Ah. Okay. That sounds good to me. Carpe diem, I'll remember that. Maybe use it the next time I stop someone for speeding." And he laughed. He was having fun thinking about it.

"I would probably not recommend it if I were you. The lawbreaker might take it that you mean seize the escape instead of seize the day. Tricky, ya know."

"You're right. I'll keep it between us. Hey, on another note, I went to see Ellis Walker at the hospital today. She's in tough shape. With all the softball games each summer, I know all the nurses in the hospital. They let me in to see her for a couple of minutes. All those ladies are so nice to me. Well, she didn't have much to say, kind of drugged up, but did mumble something about Michael and a dog. She seemed very upset with what had happened but vague on the details. Then she drifted off to sleep."

Bart hesitated. Not hearing any comment from Phoebe, he continued. "Then the lead charge nurse came in. She told me I had to leave and invited me for a cup of coffee. I was feeling kind of wore out, but took her up on the offer anyway. I was hoping to get some info on her patient. Did I tell you about this nurse? Diane's a really great person and we had a fun visit, reminiscing about the days she was the star pitcher on the Bedpans softball team."

Phoebe heard this and felt a pang of jealousy. To the casual observer it would have been more than a pang, closer to a jolt. She thought of the black negligee and decided right then and there she needed to up her game.

Time to order number two—black, short, and sexy. *Brace yourself Bart. I'm not ready for someone else to buy you coffee.*

DOGGY TREATS

Sitting on the radiant heated front porch, all wrapped up in their winter duds, Augusta and Queennie were sharing their thoughts on the art of snowmobiling in the winter and talking about a motorcycle purchase for Augusta for summer options. The newly acquired dog, Fido, was resting on the floor on his heated doggy bed between the two of them. The ladies were spoiling him beyond reason until the rightful owner could be determined. Queennie lived in Pikeview. Old Al's passing had brought her and her motorcycle riding friends to Oresville for the memorial service. Augusta and Queennie had become steadfast friends from that meeting.

She changed the subject to neighborhood talk. "You know Queennie, I've had enough of these neighbors complaining about every little thing, like a mule and a dog. After all, this is the Higgins house, the biggest and oldest on the street. And, it's been here longer than any of their little abodes."

"Totally right, Augusta. But no one lives in mansions like this anymore. It costs a fortune to heat the things and big families are out of favor even with the Catholic Church. But let's not go there." She chuckled at this thought.

"I know you're correct, but still, I was here first. Well, not me, but Grandma Connie had it built or the Higgins family had it built for her. I was thinking they probably built it for her to stay away from Omaha. She was quite the woman. You'd be lucky to stay out of her way, for sure. Oh, and some young guy dropped by today to see his dog, Fido. Nice fella and asked if I could keep it until he finds a place to live that'll have space for it to run. Normally I would not get crosswise with a dog and its owner, but this is temporary. If I wanted a pet, I'd have one already. Not keen on what you got us into, Queennie."

"Hey, I was just trying to help. I pray someone would do the same for me if ever needed. Right? It's what good people do. Agree?" She gave a questioning look to Augusta.

Augusta gave her a thoughtful stare then looked out over the frozen front yard. She was thinking about the comment. "Do ya think so?"

"Absolutely. What does it hurt? Not a thing. I'll take him home to Pikeview if he's on thin ice with you."

"He's fine. After only one day I'm getting used to him, but I had to put a little step ladder to my mattress for him. Not much of a jumper for as big as he is. I don't think he is just a Labrador. He must be mixed with something way bigger."

"I thought Fido was the woman's dog—from yesterday. How is it this guy's dog now?"

Hearing his name, Fido perked up his ears to take in the talk, hoping this gig was not nearing an end. Sensing the conversation was not threatening to his current comfort level, he went back to sleep with a huff.

"He didn't bother to explain and I didn't ask. Mind your own business, ya know. He offered to pay for lodging and food until he could care for him. Of course, I told him not to worry. Fido seems to be learning a great deal from Rose. If he stays here, I intend to give him a real name fit for a dog."

Queennie wisely chose to ignore the renaming of the dog. "If this dog starts braying like Rose, your neighbors will have more than a hissy fit. I can see Onis Adams at the door already."

"Too damn bad is what I say. My house, my rules. They can get over it."

"Agreed, Augusta. After all, these animals need a place to live too. And I think they're cute. I'd call it 'active storage.' You're keeping them temporarily until a permanent home can be found, if ever."

"I like that term. It sounds about right for the time being. Active storage. I think I'll use it on Stoker the postmistress and our town magistrate, Ovis. He's a study— been retired in place for years."

Queennie was hoping to refresh Augusta on her status regarding the mule, "I'm on record as 'not interested in taking ownership of Albert's braying pet,' correct? Rose was not much of a pet per se, but Albert loved her. They kept each other company in the mountains above Oresville, and Rose didn't bother anyone because there was no one to bother. On the other hand, I live on the west end of Pikeview. It's eclectic for sure, and we all tolerate each other's differences. A pet mule in the yard might be the proverbial straw, ya think?"

At this observation, she let loose with a hearty laugh. The thought of what her neighbors would say presented an entertaining picture. With a great sense of humor, she could easily add a lighter view to a serious discussion. She could laugh with, not at, human nature or redefine a happening with humor, sometimes inappropriately. But she was a kind, considerate, generous person. It was easy to overlook a misplaced laugh occasionally. These last few months Augusta was reluctantly learning from her how to lighten up.

One would describe Queennie as having a sturdy countenance. She was on the average side of looks, height, and intelligence, but clever to the point of inventiveness, able to solve any problem with a work around—replacement was never a first choice. As a radiator shop owner and worker, she had the strength of a thirty-year old weightlifter, and walked with a confident swagger that put to shame the average sixty-year-old man or woman.

"You might think they're cute but the mailman thinks differently. Did you know they won't deliver mail to my house as long as Rose is in the front yard?"

"You've got to be kidding. I thought nothing stopped the mail being delivered, the rain, sleet, snow thing."

"Yea, well that might be true in the big cities, but here in little ol' Oresville, the postman does what he pleases with the full backing of that crazy bitch, Postmaster Lyla Stoker. Pardon my French."

"So noted. How about I go in and fix us a hot toddy. Just to help us get over this aggravation."

"Stellar idea, Queennie. And bring that wool blanket that's over the sofa. Between that and the toddy we should be toasty warm."

Queennie sauntered into the house. Augusta snuggled down in a lightweight blanket, eased the wooden rocking chair into motion, and wrapped a long red scarf around her neck. She looked around the yard and thought, *Enjoy it now, because mother and Uncle Q will be moving in soon. They're at Q's house for now, but it's more of a little cabin. When their furnishings arrive from Europe, they'll be delivered to this house. I need to decide where I want to live until the summer. They had it jacked, enjoying life in France, not caring a whit what was going on here. Then they return and announce they'd be living here. What about me? It's always about them.*

All this thinking without a solution was tiring, and she tried some deep breathing to empty her mind. Just then Augusta had a burst of thought about Al's gold. She felt a bit of chagrin over keeping it or using it or giving it to Queennie. Now that the two of them were friends, it was tough to keep silent about it. She had packed it up before setting the cabin on fire months ago. The gold-filled pickle jars were safely stashed here in a kitchen cupboard. Technically it was her family's cabin and Al was a rent-free guest. Possession is nine tenths of the law was a handy rationalization. Now that she had become good friends with Al's wife, Queennie, it could be said that it belonged to her. At the most awkward of times, it was the elephant in the room of her thinking.

The fragrance of lemon and honey in the infused special tea crawled into her sinuses before Queennie arrived with the toddys. She told herself, *Oh well, I'll figure it out later,* and sank back into the rocker, bundled up against the freezing temperature.

Queennie arrived with insulated mugs for each of them, "You look deep in thought."

"I am. I'm so angry at my mother. Uncle Q, not so much. They just waltz on back to Oresville, decide to take over the family homestead, and it's up to me to figure out a new place to live. When summer breaks, I'll move back to the trailer at the Last. Planning for summer doesn't solve the immediate winter problem. It's just unfair and thoughtless of her."

"Hold your horses. You're almost whining. Think of it this way. It's her house and they're on the old side of life. This place is crowded already. Now envision all of their stuff from Europe. Why it'll be so tight nobody will have the space to fart!"

Augusta had to laugh at this thought, "You're probably right. It'll be a challenge to put one more stick of furniture in this place."

"Exactly. It's much easier for them to stay here and you find another place to live. Your family owns more than half the buildings and property in town. You can use this as an excuse to remodel one of your properties on Main Street. Go after space on a top floor, combine two units, huge windows, golden afternoon light, the perfect mountain views. You would be able to look at Mt. Massive anytime of the day or night, if there was snow reflecting the moon. It could be a great place to start fresh, right?"

"I could do that. It would be fun to have a new project. I need something to get through the long months until summer."

Queennie continued, "In the meanwhile, how about you come down to Pikeview and stay with me. It's lower in elevation and the weather is temperate most days. Not like up here at 10-5. My home isn't a mansion like this one, but it has three bedrooms, a sizeable garage for my toys, and lots of room in the kitchen. We could have some fun cooking and entertaining my motorcycle buddies. When the weather's good we can take off on local rides to catch breakfast or lunch somewhere."

"I only keep the shop open until Thursday. The long weekend keeps my employees happy and turnover is zip. First quarter of this year I started partnering with the high schools and the community college for internships. Bringin' in the young kids keeps the place jumpin' with their music and friends stopping' by. The old guys like teaching them the trade. The other shops in town work with me. We guarantee the kids a job when they graduate if the mentor we assign them to is happy. Not everyone is supposed to go to college, but most school districts have not figured this out."

Augusta was listening hard to this, considering the incredible offer. Queennie smiled with a long lingering look and added, "I'd love your company."

Augusta was not surprised at this generous offer coming from Queennie. It could be short term and solve the living questions facing her if she were to start a remodel project. Living in Pikeview, Augusta would be closer to Hank Williams. She could follow his activities and encourage him to finish school. At the same time, she could get to know his wacky family. Maybe. Queennie owned her own business, and would be gone most days, leaving Augusta to her precious time alone. The real capper would be some added distance between her and Mother. "Let me think on this, Queennie. I really appreciate the offer, but you know how I feel about leaving my mountains."

There it was again—a spark of the vision of those damn pickle jars in the kitchen.

PARTY ON, ORESVILLE

Christmas Eve finally arrived and the Club was decorated to the nines. Roz had made sure that everything was in place, ready for the guests to arrive. The twelve-foot high, locally harvested pine tree stood at attention in the main room, lit with a thousand colorful, twinkling lights.

All of the decorations near the top of the tree were in place thanks to people using stepladders, but the lower branches were awaiting the special touch of the Oresville children to finish the trimming. Over the years, the Club had established a process to decorate the tree by age groups. The little ones 'just walking' up to the age of three decorated the lowest limbs of the giant tree. This group was referred to as the Entry Level. Those children, four years of age to six decorated the next several limbs. Those over six years of age were the helpers and were put in charge of the little ones, handling the plastic balls for each child to place on the tree. The kids at the double digits in age, starting at ten were the bosses to supervise, decorate the mid-level of the tree, and present the finished product to the adults in the room.

No cell phones could be used until the tree was completely decorated when all kids were posed for the annual Oresville Children's Photo. The action continued when Santa arrived at exactly five-thirty in the early evening. Each child got to talk with him, a photo was snapped by the parents, and a gift was bestowed from the giant gift bags that were hauled in before St. Nick's arrival.

Brian Friedrich, the Club bartender, decorated the club's bar area immediately after Thanksgiving. He draped tinsel from strands of blue lights across the back of the bar area. This had the effect of an early festive atmosphere for the entire month of December and encouraged visits by even the grumpiest Scrooges among the members.

As the guests started arriving at four o'clock in the afternoon to kick off their Christmas Eve, a spirit of excitement filled the air. With the coordination of all details left to Roz, the party person, each and every man, woman and child was gratified to be surrounded by a sparkle in the atmosphere, imagined or real. They would begin the holiday celebrations here at the Club, then move to their respective homes to continue into the evening.

Phoebe had lucked into a set of circumstances resulting in her working the six to two shift. She arrived at the Club early enough to help Roz with the setup, tree decorations, and the potluck table. She was decked out in a red sweater with her favorite narrow-leg jeans tucked into Doc Martens. With an inseam of thirty-six inches, she resembled a team member of Santa's reindeer, and decided to add a band of antlers holding back her thick, naturally wavy, chestnut brown hair. For a touch of fun, her ears supported rings of Christmas tree balls that let out a jingle when she moved, similar to a bell on a cat. Never one to overdo on the makeup, she had brushed glitter over her cheeks and some flakes were occasionally sliding to the sweater, catching the light, adding sparkle to her chest that would otherwise be cinched up behind a bulletproof vest. Phoebe admired this rather festive touch with the added sensation of something new—eagerness for a new year.

Carrie Jean wandered in and immediately perched on a stool at the bar. She was all smiles. Her crazy curly, shiny, red hair was looking unusually wild, mirroring the light show at her neck. She appeared to be dressed in an outfit that matched Brian's. These two seemed to have the same fashion sense. Was something going on here beyond a friends-with-benefits fling? Her friends first noticed something more serious last August when Carrie Jean and Brian first showed up for Old Al's memorial service in matching scarf and tie. They had not said much, but they were seeing one another whenever the opportunity presented itself. Carrie Jean was not a person to talk about relationships, fashion, nor the routine occurrences in life—unless it resulted in a hot news lead for her baby, the e-Blast!

The local thrift store had a wide assortment of festive personal decor. Carrie Jean and Brian had a good time trying on different sets of lights. While Brian had chosen a flashing bowtie, she had settled on multiple circles of white lights at her neck—simple yet elegant at a level that even white pearls would never match. Wearing the usual black leggings, barely sufficient canvas Toms on her feet, and a red sweatshirt, she was ready for the evening. The top was her costume for the Ugly Sweater competition. It depicted a group of reindeer gathered at a bar. Christmas Eve minus one on a nearby calendar, and they were voting on "Go or No Go" with heavy snow raging outside as seen through the nearby window. She wore the same shirt every year for this contest and had yet to win. It promised to be a fun evening with or without the bragging rights for this year's contest.

The regulars wandered into the Club. They sat at the far end of the bar, along the curve that finished the bar at the wall, like a team ready for the play to be announced. They were people with varying backgrounds and circumstances. Dressed alike in a weak effort of red and green for the holiday, they were drawn to the Club as a social outlet for an otherwise quiet, uneventful life. The Moly Mine was a solid way to earn a living as their families had for many decades, but for some it was a flatline kind of work. Many of them were retired or retired in place, counting down the days until it was official.

Shoulder to shoulder, like sailors at the sunset ceremony for the lowering of the colors, the regulars sat at the bar. Brian had set them up with the Drink of the Month. The current DOM was called Rudolph's Nose—hot chocolate and peppermint schnapps, topped with lots of whipped cream, shaved dark chocolate, and a bright Chelan Cherry on top. It was straight from Sheriff Joe's drink journal created when he was his mom and dad's favorite bartender.

For Joe's fortieth birthday he donated his drink diary to the Club. Since then, Brian featured a special *Sheriff Joe's Drink of the Month*. As an adult, Joe seldom drank anything other than non-alcoholic beer. Willie made sure the best NA was stocked for the sheriff.

These recipes were translated from the awkward early printing in his drink journal at the age of four to Joe's beautiful cursive penmanship as a teenager. The Club members turned out the first of every month to critique Brian's beverage selection. Club manager, Willie, Brian's dad, would set the price. He would jack up the price for these special drinks for the first half of the month and then lower it gradually through the last half. This was a pricing strategy he had learned from careful scrutiny of shopping promotions predicated by *Blue Light Specials* designed to attract bargain shoppers in stores. These specially priced products weren't as special as they were abundant.

Willie had advertised a four o'clock start for the Christmas Eve Happy Hour. Bartender Brian, decked out with a lighted tie, had added a furry Santa hat at the last minute. The regulars concluded that he looked like a Santa Elf albeit his six foot plus height. Augusta was wearing an over-the-top ugly sweater and would probably win this year's competition—again. She enjoyed this party at the club and spent months online shopping for the winning sweater. Queennie, in Christmas leathers, was enjoying this first Christmas Eve with her new-found friends. Undersheriff Bill Diamond joined the group, followed by Phoebe, her tasks completed.

Bill was dressed in his usual attire of straight leg jeans, cowboy boots, a madras shirt, with a faded red holiday decor vest. He usually joined family friends in the meeting room, but his recent interest in Roz brought him to a bar stool. As he sat down, he noticed the back of the bar was all mirrors. This prompted a quick check of his reflection. He could not help but run fingers through his hair for the fresh tousled look of a male cologne model. Then, a serious frown check, straight-on at the mirror, followed with a quick turn of his face each way for that charming profile.

Augusta watched the Bill Diamond primping ceremony with a smile. With a wink and a nod to Brian, "Time for a toast," she declared.

Phoebe chimed in, "Wait. Let's get Roz here too."

Just then Roz came out of the swinging kitchen doors, sauntering on red patent leather high heels, no longer covered in a frilly holiday apron. Despite the Ugly Sweater contest, Roz was decked out in a low-cut, form fitting, sequined red dress, her shiny black hair falling to her shoulders, and makeup done perfectly. She looked to be a true Louisiana Diva.

Bill nearly fell out of his chair. *Is this the woman who sits at our front desk every day? She's always lovely, but tonight she's luscious. Those beautiful brown eyes, that curly black hair, the long, lean body wrapped in brazen red. How is it I never noticed this incredible woman? Maybe our recent tete-e-tete is not just Friends with Benefits as we had each assumed.*

It was at this nanosecond, Bill Diamond's epiphany of love hit him like a train. He had always believed that one would grow into love for another. The Shakespearean *suddenly in love* was a literary hallucination. Not humanly possible, but this was an *aha moment*. He could not take his eyes off her, mouth slightly opened with realization that time could stand still when least expected. He choked out one word, "Roz?" Then snapped back to attention, slid off the bar stool, and dragged another one over for her to sit between Phoebe and him.

"Hi everyone. Is it time for a drink?" Roz settled into the stool Bill offered.

Bill quickly put his arm around her back, "Does anyone have a sprig of mistletoe handy?"

A chuckle rippled around the bar top and with that comment, the party officially began.

Augusta was admiring her friend, Roz, dressed as always *appropriately plus* for whatever occasion, "We were just waiting for you. You look fabulous. I take it you're not participating in the ugly sweater contest this year? Is there a significant other going to surprise us this Christmas?"

"Nah. Just like to dress up. You know me, always ready just in case that fabulous single guy should wander in." She winked double at Bill, nudged against his ribs, and awarded him with the Roz Smile that could light up all of Oresville.

Augusta had ordered up a round for everyone seated at the bar. Brian deposited a freshly prepared Sazerac in front of Roz and double checked to see that everyone's glass was full. He poured himself one short shot of Augusta's Pappy Van Winkle Bourbon and turned to her.

"We're ready for that toast now."

Augusta lifted her glass as did everyone else.

"Merry Christmas to each and every one. May we remember the reason we're celebrating, be grateful for this lovely evening, and enjoy the company of all gathered here. Salute!"

"Cheers," came the chorus of friends as they all took a sip.

"And here's to the coming new year." chimed in Phoebe who had plans for a new direction in her life.

The late afternoon passed into early evening. The children completed the Christmas tree decorations, the Club Annual Photo had been taken by fifty or so blazing cell phones. Santa passed out gifts to each child. The noise in the room was beyond the state limit, as the excitement hit another crescendo with each additional gift.

The unexpected adult gifts were the most fun. Some regulars had plotted and schemed since the Fourth of July for the special shocking, unexpected gift. From a secret admirer, Augusta had gotten a pair of knee-high socks for the women's softball team. The upper portion declared, "Takin' names and kickin butt." Augusta was the team's manager. As a tough-minded leader, some might have used the word tyrant. She had played for many years, but an unlucky slide into home plate took her out of action permanently. The team promoted her to manager—not coach. At one point, she was so upset with a no-show player, she drove to a nearby bar, pulled the supposed pitcher off the bar stool, and hauled her to practice.

Likely the same fan also treated Roz with an unexpected gift of a black sweatshirt that screamed out in neon colors on the front, clearly stated, *Shut the*... and on the back completed the usual expletive with a mellow, front *door*. It was so Roz.

Phoebe was enjoying the evening immensely after two cocktails. She had already switched up to soda with a twist of lime. After all, she had to drive herself home.

The Unexpected Gifts were continuing when Santa's helper appeared to be in on the next one and assumed a sexy, come hither voice. He called out, "Oh, Deputy Phoebe, we've got a special treat just for you. Come on over here. Visit your Santa." The most shocking gift of the evening was for Phoebe.

A touch to her face and mouth in a round "Oh," she shouted out a surprised, "Who? Me?" and slid off the bar stool. She took long steps into the meeting room, and, for the fun of it, sat on Santa's lap. Those in attendance were surprised by her good-natured display of playing along and cheered, whistled, and applauded. The helper presented a beautifully wrapped gift. She pulled the ribbon, opened the box, and inside was a flimsy, lacey, see-through red silk negligee. She held it up for all to see. Those in the room yelled out varying cries of "Ooh-La-La." Phoebe looked around the room for someone to take ownership. Carrie Jean shrugged as if to say, "No idea." Roz was standing at the doorway, crossed her arms, cranked up a conspiratorial smile, and retreated into the bar area.

The biggest surprise gift was for Carrie Jean. The not-so-secret admirer was Brian. When Santa's helper called out Carrie Jean's name with an auctioneer's voice, he ended the chant with a shout out to Brian. All those in the room quieted and waited for them to step to the twinkling tree. Santa presented the box to Brian, who slowly offered it to her. She slowly opened it, half expecting an exploding gag gift. Inside was a beautiful birthstone ring set in a gold band. She looked from Brian to Phoebe, to Roz, to Augusta, and then back to Brian, total confusion reigned on her face.

Brian was laughing, "We should get married and decorate our own Christmas trees forever."

This was more of a statement than a question and Carrie Jean was staring at him. For once in her life, she was speechless. His comment started to sink in and she was flummoxed for a sentence. Only singular words came out, "Right. Right. RIGHT." The Oresville community gathered in the Club meeting room let out a cheer and started clapping. From his six-foot five-inch frame, he leaned down to her barely five-foot stature, grabbed her, twirled her around, and the whole room started laughing. They would make quite the couple. Later Brian would admit that she was the only one who didn't know about this in advance. As bylines go, Brian got this one.

'TWAS THE NIGHT BEFORE

Parents were gathering up their families in hopes of getting the kids to bed early. The remaining club members sat at the bar and decided they would have one more drink before they called the end to the night.

Just then the phone behind the bar started to ring.

"We're having a great Christmas Eve celebration at 10-5. Brian speaking."

Brian always liked to announce to a caller what was happening at the Club, easy and inexpensive marketing. Adding the 10-5 represented the high altitude of Oresville, although Oresville actually sat somewhat lower at 10-3 or so.

"Hey Brian, this is Billy over at the towing yard. I just got the truck in tonight from the event up at Slide Lake.

One last thing before I drive over to Denver tomorrow to celebrate. Is Phoebe hanging out there tonight?"

"Sure is. Let me get her for ya."

Putting his hand over the phone receiver, Brian nodded toward Phoebe. "Call for you."

Brian stretched the phone cord over to where she was seated. "Phoebe here."

"Hey, Merry Christmas. Billy here. Just wanted you to know I finally got that red pickup from No Name Gulch into the yard. It took some extra time to bring in the right tow machine for recovery. I found a journal of some sort under the front seat but nothing else. No luggage, no purse—nada."

"Okay. Can I stop over tomorrow to get it? I'm working the holiday morning shift."

"Nope. No one will be around. Everyone's on call for this one day of the year. Tell ya what, how about I drop it at your place tonight on my way home. That'd be convenient for both of us both livin' at The Court."

"Great. How about an hour from now?"

"You got it. Later, Phoebe."

Returning the phone to Brian, she re-joined the festivities with her friends.

Only Carrie Jean seemed to overhear Phoebe's side of the conversation. "Any news on the maybe dead or worse woman?"

"Not yet, just what you heard yesterday from the so-called husband. The vehicle's at Billy's yard now."

Yesterday Carrie Jean left the county office building and ran up Main Street in hot pursuit of the woman's husband, Mickey. She could smell a headline brewing a mile away.

He was not interested in coffee with her at the Buns. In lock step with him, she pursued answers to her questions. Starting with how his dog came to be with his wife? Why were both the wife and dog in Oresville? After all, they lived in Greenstone over a hundred or so miles away. He stared straight forward, pursed his lips, and quickened his pace, adding that he needed to go see about his dog. She was not to be put off and repeated questions about where he had been this weekend. He worked days so what about after work? Finally, he stopped and said, "I told her not to go up there. As usual she didn't listen. And, she's been keeping my dog until I find a place to live in Oresville."

Listening to his one and only comment, she felt it was a lead. Answers to more questions could result in a story for the e-Blast! Ellis and the dog had to have stayed somewhere. To follow the trail first thing this morning, she started calling all the hotels in the area, asking about weekend guests with a casual question directed to their guest ledgers. She got nowhere. The hotel employees were not about to let loose with information to the local newspaper person. No siree. Carrie Jean was left with zero answers to a million questions.

The questions around this Walker person could be moved to a back burner for the evening's celebration. When

Carrie Jean heard the conversation Phoebe was having with Billy, she decided it was the right time to tell Phoebe about her suspicions that Mickey had been with his wife, Ellis, before Augusta and company ran across the accident. Otherwise, why would he say, "I told her not to go up there, but she didn't listen." That's an odd comment if he wasn't involved.

Phoebe stuck to the club and a twist, but finished the evening with a virgin Rudolf's Nose with extra whipped cream. She noticed the questioning look, "So what're ya thinkin', CJ?"

Looking away from her pal, then returning her glance, Carrie Jean confessed, "I got a comment out of the husband, Mickey, yesterday. I think it might be a lead you could use."

"Come on. You can't be serious. It's Christmas Eve, it's late, and now you tell me you have a tip about this woman. She's lying in a hospital a hundred miles away with a husband who for all intents and purposes could not care less."

"Actually, it's more like one hundred and twenty miles away. I didn't think what he said was a big deal at first, but now I'm thinkin' otherwise. You can get further on this than I did."

"What did you do?"

"I checked all the area hotels. No sign of her over the weekend."

"I can't do this. Can we wait till morning? I've got the early shift tomorrow. Let's have a good evening and I'll call you first thing. By the way, I'm so happy for you and Brian. I think Roz has already planned the wedding as a small-town celebration."

Carrie Jean laughed. "Of course she has. That's a good thing as I wouldn't know where to begin." She looked at Brian in a new light, licked her drink's topping, and caught up with the rest of the crew at the bar.

The camaraderie of this group was tenacious. Each of them was from somewhere else except Augusta who was the third generation of her family in Oresville. Although she had been married five times, and was quick to point out only three husbands, there was no one to carry on the Higgins family name. The same was true for Queennie and the jury was still out on Roz, Carrie Jean, and Phoebe. Bill Diamond had two teenage kids in Denver, living life a mile in the sky. This small town meant so much to each of them, feeling the closeness and caring everyone shared. They had all agreed that despite the occasional differences, there was no place like Oresville. Now they had a wedding to look forward to and Roz was already setting menu choices, wondering about the right flowers and possible venues.

Christmas Eve was coming to a close for these single friends. They finished their drinks and slipped on their coats. There were many well wishes called into the night. There was high anticipation of a shared Christmas

Day Cajun dinner. As they waved to each other in the parking lot, one could hear the chorus of "Merry Christmas" and "See ya tomorrow." Everyone was in high spirits, looking forward to tomorrow's dinner party.

It was almost daylight with the full moon. The snow on Mount Massive has clearly outlined in moonlight. It was a dry cold night. The air was sharp and snow crunched with each step. Despite the amazing setting, Phoebe's mood dimmed as she drove. *Alone again. Wish Bart didn't have to work today and tomorrow. I'd like to have spent Christmas with him. Wonder if he feels the same way? Maybe I'll just call him and see what he's up to. I can just say I am calling to wish him a Merry Christmas. After all, we're friends, aren't we?*

The trailer house felt especially empty as she entered. She decided it was a perfect night to plug in the outside strand of colorful lights on the rented trailer. With this lumination reflected through the window, her mood lightened. Without second guessing herself, she shed her coat, pulled up a chair and dialed Bart. She just needed to hear his voice and see how his day had gone.

Recognizing her number, he skipped past the Officer Masterson announcement and went directly to, "Merry Christmas, Phoebe."

"And a Merry Christmas to you too. Thought I'd give you a call and see how things are going on patrol."

"All's quiet, which is great. Hope it continues through tomorrow."

"Me too. Too bad we both have to work—you on patrol and me on call."

"Well, that's just what we singles do, right?"

"Right."

"So, Phoebe, how'd the Christmas Eve celebration go at the Club? Anything special happen?"

Asking this question, Bart was wondering about his surprise gift. It had been left up to Roz to choose something appropriate. His thinking was a high-end vacuum cleaner or maybe a pink toilet brush. He was hesitant about these two ideas and reached out to Roz who gladly stepped up to the request. He had talked with Roz on county business and trusted her judgement in choosing just the right gift. She had called him, leaving a short message saying he would like what she had picked out.

Bart sensed a relationship with Phoebe could go beyond the occasional phone call, diner dinner in Greenstone, or a ride to an ER. His last girlfriend turned into a real train wreck and left a dark spot on his heart. They were carefully growing their friendship, each skittish about the opposite sex.

Many months ago, Bart had called the Green County Sheriff's office to share information about Old Al's estranged wife. Roz had answered. When hearing this man's deep, rolling, confidential tone, she slipped into a flirtatious modus operandi, and shared that Deputy Phoebe was not around. She was available to help.

From this start back in August, it felt like he knew Roz and could comfortably call her for help with this gift idea. Being the fun person she was, Roz happily agreed to assist. After a call or two they decided a "Club unexpected gift" could be bought and delivered as a real surprise. Phoebe was great at never being caught off guard and Roz was looking for the "window of opportunity" to reverse this trend.

Bart wanted to make up for the Fat Lip Disaster from his first date with Phoebe at Mo's Diner. The trip to the hospital was memorable and they shared some laughs over it now that her lip had healed without a scar, but he knew he could do better. Roz had agreed and came up with the idea of something "fun" in her words. So, she did the buying and he sent the money. Easy Peasey.

With Bart's comment, a thought popped up in Phoebe's head. *What's that question about the events at the Club supposed to mean? Is he fishing for a "something special?" What would he care about what happened? Maybe he's just making conversation.*

"Yes. My best friend, CJ, got engaged to Brian, the Club's bartender. We're all so happy for both of them."

"Nice, but did anything else special happen?"

"Well, I told you that there are special secret gifts given out. I got one that was quite a shock."

"What was it?"

"A see-through red negligee. Must have come from Roz. Or maybe CJ."

"Well, actually, it was from me. I called Roz at the Sheriff's office and asked her for help with a special gift for you. She guaranteed it would happen. I hope you like it."

Phoebe was flabbergasted. *A red sexy nightgown? Oh, leave it to Roz to come up with this number.*

"Yes, I did. It's great and thank you so much. I promise to model it for you. How thoughtful you are. Now I feel bad that I didn't get you a gift." *I cannot believe I just offered to model it—pure slut mode! Where did that come from?*

"Not to worry Phoebe. There could be plenty of time for gifts."

What'd he mean by that? I'm over-thinking every comment. Is it because he's the first guy in years I am willing to risk my heart over? I don't think I can do another Disaster Relationship like in SL-ICK. Bart seems different. Take it easy, girl, and let this relationship unfold. The lacey bedroom numbers will help move things along on New Year's Eve, maybe set the tone for next year. Let's hope.

Just then the doorbell rang.

"Sorry Bart, gotta go. The towing operator did his usual once-over on what he towed off the mountain. He found a book under the front seat and is dropping it off. Again, thanks for the wonderful gift. I look forward to trying it on for you. Merry Christmas."

"What? I missed what you said, can you repeat? Phoebe, wait. Hold on. Don't hang up."

"Gotta run, Sweetie. Later." She disconnected and chuckled at how she left poor ol' Ponytail Guy hanging. She could tell he was smiling by the end of the call.

She opened the front door to Billy standing on the front steps, looking the worse for wear. No sign of the holidays on his coveralls or ball cap. It was after eight at night, temps were way below freezing, and he had the look of a small business owner working on Christmas Eve. It's tough doing business in a small town. There's hardly enough work for several employees and continuous work for the owner. When there's a no-show employee, the owner must jump into the wrecker to keep the customer service side going.

"Hi, Phoebe. Here's the book. Hope it helps with the work you're doin' on this case. There doesn't seem to be any mechanical malfunction but it took quite a crash and the frame's bent. No wonder the rescue guys had to use a pry bar to get the driver's side door open. The passenger side is crushed in from where it landed against the huge lodgepole pines. She must have been flyin' up that forest road from the looks of it. Plus, the tires were nearly bald and that's bad on any road. I'm surprised she got up that far. Oh, and by the way the clock stopped at one twenty-four if that makes any difference."

"Thanks so much for doing this on Christmas Eve, Billy. Safe travels and a Merry Christmas to ya."

"You too. Bye."

She stood at the opened door as Billy climbed into his ride and idled off in the direction of his own trailer house a few blocks away. She was thinking he did not look anywhere close to having any holiday spirit. The air was dry with the temperature close to zero and humidity in the single digits. A quick inhale through one's nostrils would crystallize the smallest amount of moisture in a nose. The stars were a sweep of sparkling white dots across the sky, dimmed by the rising waxing gibbous moon, ready to be full tomorrow.

Maybe she should have invited Billy in for coffee or a sandwich. There was not anything stocked for entertaining and barely necessities for any day. Phoebe ate most meals out or leaned against the countertop and did a smear on a soda cracker for a late-night snack. Bart's visit was another week away and she'd worry later about stocking food for the visit.

She sat down at her kitchen table with the newly found book. Opening it and looking at the first page, she could see this was a diary. More importantly, the owner was Ellis Walker of Greenstone. Name and town neatly printed on the fly page with a start date twelve months ago at the first of this year. It looked as though she was not making daily entries, but hit or miss on a day here, a week there. Phoebe scanned to the last few pages and could see an entry every hour. It started when she awoke in the cab with a splitting headache, truck off the road, a total whiteout beyond the vehicle, and wondering what happened.

Phoebe was wide awake fast. This was an incredible narrative. Each entry gave a description of what she was experiencing hour by hour. The handwriting became more and more garbled and it was clear that Ellis was declining fast. The entries noted that she had Type I diabetes and was without insulin. As a result, her health was failing, it was bitter cold, and the dog was the only thing keeping her warm. The passenger door was wedged against pine trees. The driver's door was jammed or something and the notes described how she kicked at the door and windows with no result. Her notes included remorse when it came to how she treated her husband, Michael.

She had gone off the road on Sunday afternoon. The weather was good, but the episode left her unconscious. When she came to it was cold, the weather was in full out storm mode, and the engine would not turn over. She did not have extra clothes and no food. Phoebe felt horrified by the notes and the agony of this woman's experience. Had it not been for Augusta's snowmobile club on Tuesday morning, she certainly would have died.

What brought this woman to Green County, wondered Phoebe. She flipped back several pages in the journal to the notes starting on Sunday morning. Ellis was writing self-affirmations as part of her anger management program. The list of bullet points was titled Tips for Taming My Anger. Number four advised her to step away from what was happening, take a time-out. *So, this is why she was on the Forest Service road by herself, no extra warm clothing, and no food or insulin. Something must have happened on Sunday to cause her to drive up the Wurtz Ditch trail. I wonder if she was taking part in TuTu's counseling sessions this past weekend.* Clearly, she had not planned a drive to Slide Lake. The unfortunate mishap was just that, poor judgement and little experience with the demands of high mountain switchbacks. Bringing the dog with her for the weekend was logical since it was something longer than a day trip.

Phoebe believed the dog was a key element in this case. Why would Mickey refer to it as my dog and it ended up in the truck with Ellis? Then Carrie Jean confessed that the husband told her something about, "I told her not to go up there." These two pieces of information put them together at some point over the weekend. Mickey lied.

I'm going to track down Mickey and get the sequence of events out of him. This was her last thought before she fell asleep at the rented trailer's kitchen table.

Ho-Ho-Ho

Phoebe was the first and only one in the patrol room at six in the morning. It was Christmas Day and historically quiet. Several other deputies were assigned half-pay-on-call without the need to come into the county offices. With no kids or family to celebrate Christmas morning, Phoebe always volunteered to cover the office. At the end of the morning shift she planned to go directly to Roz's to help with the dinner.

There was a satisfying atmosphere of closeness among the Sheriff's staff whether or not there were people in the offices. As she sat in the patrol room, Phoebe had a sense of urgency to move the day forward.

The County's emergency lines were all transferred to a central dispatch unit for the county and it was stone quiet without all the usual business of a week day. The lights on the patrol room Christmas tree were on with an occasional sparking, a real distraction. She refrained from starting the interoffice holiday music over the paging system. At the one month mark the music was an irritant and did nothing to keep people in the holiday spirit. The gift shopping was completed and even the thrift store was closed for any last-minute purchases. The usual holiday overeating would reach a crescendo today without a final stop at the grocery. By this time tomorrow morning, Christmas would be over and the exhausted celebrants would turn their focus to plotting, scheming and creating their usual blown out of all proportion New Year's resolutions.

Before leaving on patrol, Phoebe was trying to make sense of what Carrie Jean had said about Mickey. *Best thing I can do is use the driver's license photo Roz pulled up and visit the local motels and see if anyone can remember seeing Ellis. If she was here for the weekend, why no suitcase? If she had a suitcase, where is it now? The dog was Mickey's dog or so he said, yet it was with her on Tuesday morning. Hubby doesn't want to talk about her and she's in a hospital and can't talk. This whole circumstance is sketchy.*

After researching credit card charges for Ellis Walker or Michael Walker, Roz had left Phoebe a note saying she had gotten nothing back yet, but would take another run at it on Monday. Phoebe locked the back door to the parking lot, stepped over to today's ride and scraped the windows on the Sheriff's Wrangler. With no one around to notice for the better, she had decided she would enjoy driving the tricked out four by four on this special day.

It was a clear and crisp day and the sky was getting bright over the eastern peaks. The temperatures would not get higher than a balmy ten, maybe fifteen degrees and with no wind the day would be tolerable. At an altitude over ten thousand feet, winters were always cold, the sun was weak from November until April, and the absence of wind was a big event. Delighted with this spotless ride, she opened the driver's door, stepped easily to the high floorboard, shifted her bullet proof vest into a halfway level of comfort, and spun the tires exiting the parking lot. Might as well enjoy the ride before the townsfolk are up and observing her untoward behavior.

Her first and second stops at the local motels yielded nothing. The front desk people looked to be working double shifts. They had little interest in listening to Phoebe, looking at the driver's license photo, or checking out the weekend ledger information she was fishing for. The lone person at each place appeared to have perfected the art of sleeping with their eyes open. Anyone working on this holiday could be excused for their wide-eyed look of 'failure to connect,' fumbled words, and general disinterest.

The Sheriff's patrol was expected to scan the businesses in town on the night shift every day and first thing on the early shift when the magistrate was off-duty. They scanned the storefronts and cruised the alleyways for any signs of something that didn't look kosher. This is where the gut instinct of training, experience, and genetics of suspicious attitudes came in handy.

It was Christmas morning and Onis Adams, Oresville's magistrate, was resting comfortably at home. He would usually be checking the businesses on Main Street as this was a weekday. But not today. The town had only one law officer, Onis. No need to spend city money on an entire police force when the routine stuff could be handled by one hired hand, leaving the rest up to Sheriff Joe's patrol people.

The town's magistrate took his work less than seriously. After a forty-year career, having seen about everything there was to see at all levels of law enforcement, Onis announced he would retire on his sixty-sixth birthday next year. He worked the weekdays, forty-five weeks a year and observed all of the federal holidays. The locals were tuned into this calendar and restricted their law breaking to weekends when the Sheriff's patrol officers were keeping a lazy eye on the speeders and other scofflaws.

Onis's father had a great love for history and the state of Colorado. When his first born arrived, he took advantage of this influential position as father and insisted this son be named Onis to go with the last name of Adams.

As Onis paced through the grades of the Oresville school system, the fellow students nicknamed him Anus as a quick turn of phrase. It was a lifelong tag that Onis tolerated with selective hearing.

Little did these delinquent children know, Onis was named after the significant Onis-Adams treaty of 1819. As illogical as it appeared to be by current standards, the treaty not only gave Florida to America, but also settled the western edges of the Louisiana Purchase for the mountain claims in the Rocky's. As a result, parts of the Oresville area were south of the Arkansas River and with the treaty, considered to be Spanish turf. In 1848, that land was then relinquished to Mexico. The take away from this lesson was depending upon where you lived in Oresville, you could be on Spanish land or Mexican soil. Any land east of the river in town had a longer history of being American territory. Onis liked to lecture on this little known reason for his name when enjoying more than a few specials of the day at the Club.

At a safe ten miles an hour, in the morning half-light of seven thirty, Phoebe idled forward along the deserted Main Street. The back room lights at the Buns Up were on. For this particular holiday, the Buns would not be opening and early morning lights in the back area were unexpected. Just a quick check to confirm suspicions, she parked in the back alley and tried the door to be sure it was safely locked—surprisingly it opened to the back hallway.

She was met with a blast of the heat, cranked up music, and yelled, "Hey, Sheriff's Department, anybody here?"

The sixties and seventies rock music was dialed down; then a rustling and steps coming out of the kitchen. The owner, Rebecca Riney, was walking towards Phoebe, wiping her hands on a kitchen towel, red for the holidays. She looked relaxed in jeans, flannel shirt, boots, and the flour coated chef's coat.

"Just me, Phoebe. Couldn't sleep past my usual three a.m. alarm and decided why not get a jump on the weekend specials. Some bread can be proofed and stored in the fridge."

"Wow, my mind turns to mush with the aroma of fresh baked bread."

"Come on in and we'll share a quick cup and a taste treat. Celebrate the holiday. On me."

They moved into the kitchen and sat at the chef's table in chairs that had been there for as many years as the 1880's building. Phoebe adjusted her vest and carefully took a seat, "I can't stay long. Lots of morning checks still to do."

"I understand. I'm indulging in a little holiday Mimosa. Some friends will be stopping by later for dinner and we'll switch to brandy eggnog. A touch of the bubbly kicks it up a notch to get things started in the right direction. Especially when I serve it in the German Nachtmann crystal that's been in my family for generations."

"One of these holidays I'll get to try it, but not this one. Thanks anyway."

Rebecca nodded and set a coffee and a beautiful pastry in front of Phoebe on English Spode Christmas china. Rebecca knew how to serve those lucky enough to be at her Chef's Table. Phoebe was the only guest this early in the day, but she could imagine what it would look like by the time Rebecca's friends gathered.

"These are yesterday's Danish, but tasty with a quick warmup on the stove. I use a wood stove for my baking and the heat from it does a nice job of warming delicate pastries. It helps keep a check on my utility bill and is probably offset with the constant supply of all the wood I burn through each month."

Rebecca had a fun perspective on life. Baking had always been her passion and she was the original owner of Becky's Buns Up which opened thirty years ago. The native Oresvillians had shortened the establishment to Becky's Place and the newcomers called it the Buns. A subtle way of keeping track of the residents—original or transplant.

Phoebe almost let out a groan with deep satisfaction at the taste of this woman's magic. "You have a special touch when it comes to baking. This is over the top. I can barely boil water."

"Thanks, it seems to be genetic. My grandma and momma baked like this on a six-plate cast iron stove. It had been in the family in Germany. Great Grandma brought it with her when the family came over and landed in Keokuk, Iowa. Of course, that stove is long gone."

The story of the Riney's migration from parts of Europe to America and onto Colorado was not unusual in Oresville. Mining was a big draw for those wanting to explore, strike it rich, and be their own person. The reality was that while there were plenty of opportunities, it was a life of hardship and disgusting working conditions, with a minuscule margin for success.

The cemetery in Oresville had a hidden section of unmarked graves with thousands of bodies of Irish immigrants. Brave men and women who ventured west in the 1880s. For many of the Irish descendants in Oresville today, there was a memory, a tale, a bible carrying an inscription from the ancestor who came west only to give their life for the bloodline that would follow. Rebecca was the granddaughter of one of these Irish immigrants who left Iowa farming for the promise of a better life. Born to the son of one of these immigrants and a newly arrived German woman, Becky was a true Oresville native.

Rebecca held some kind of a record for decorating Focaccia Bread in the state of Colorado. However, she would never leave the state to compete in the contest on a national level. Denver was far enough to spend one night away from the Buns Up. There was plenty of grumbling about a person winning the state recognition and then refusing to go to the national runoff. On the bright side though, the person who came in second place always got to represent Colorado. It worked for the women who competed and the organizers could just suck it up. The Riney's were a strong minded, red-headed family of Irish descent and once Rebecca's mind was made up, it was final.

Phoebe finished the pastry and held back on the desire to lick the plate. "My Mom never cooked. I was thinking I might buy a cookbook one of these years."

"Never mind that. You have to love good food and let your mind do the rest of it. Recipes are just another person's idea of food combinations." Rebecca was speaking for herself with this advice. She was smart as a whip, creative beyond the usual, and wrapped it all in a humble attitude.

"You're here every day, seven days a week?"

"Oh yes. One or two workers for the front counter and me in the back. It's a pretty simple business plan." and she laughed at this.

Phoebe was thinking about her research on the accident and where Ellis was before Tuesday, "Were you working this last weekend?"

"Every day."

"I'm trying to track a woman who went off the road below Slide Lake, maybe Sunday or the storm on Monday. She's not from around here. Kind of unusual to be up there in the winter. Now she's in the hospital in Pikeview."

Because of the central location of her place, newsy tidbits drifted in like homing pigeons' messages. Thinking back to Sunday, Becky put two and two together and asked, "This is a longshot. Did she have a dog with her?"

"Yup, a black lab. Probably kept her alive. It's over at Augusta's now." Phoebe was thinking, *This dog keeps coming up in conversations.* She had heard of the advice to follow the money, but in this case, it's turning out to be follow the dog.

"There was a young couple and a dog here on Sunday, early afternoon. They got into an argument and I had to ask them to step outside. The other customers in the Buns were fascinated by the gal. She was talking fast, sometimes yelling, threw a napkin or two at the guy, and he just sat there. He did not look happy."

"Did she stop yelling when you asked 'em to take it outside?"

"No, she was mad. Lipped off to me and with that I told her to 'git goin.' This is a friendly coffee shop.' She stormed out, the guy looked embarrassed and took the dog to follow her. He did leave a twenty for their coffee."

"And that was it?"

Rebecca laughed at this, "Hell no. She was not done with him. They stood on the sidewalk and she continued to rip on him. Then she ran out of steam, grabbed the dog's leash, and stomped up the street to a small red pickup. Quite the excitement for a Sunday, ya know? Not exactly an afternoon delight."

LOUISIANA TANG

The rest of the morning shift gently drifted to the two o'clock cutoff time. No details were discovered from the final few hotels in town. Phoebe decided she would find Mickey tomorrow to discuss his comment to Carrie Jean, "I told her to not go up there." Phoebe was wondering if the her in this comment referred to the wife, Ellis. Mickey worked from Saturday to Wednesday each week, so if all goes according to plan, he should be at work tomorrow.

After a quick trip home to change clothes, lock up her Glock and freshen up for the festivities, Phoebe arrived at Roz's place to help with the dinner preparations. Roz loved to cook and any excuse was blown out of all proportion. By four in the afternoon all the friends would be gathered and the charcuterie board would appear to have been a success. Licked clean. Phoebe and Roz had so much to talk about: Brian and Carrie Jean's engagement, the surprise gifts at the Club party last night, and especially Phoebe's new wardrobe enhancement as instigated by the team of Ponytail Guy and Roz. Phoebe vowed to nudge Roz to see if she could get the lowdown on what was going on between her and Bill, if anything.

Roz's house was an early 1900's, relocated to Oresville when the Moly Mine started open-pit mining. To do this, the mining company moved the entire town of Climax to Oresville. All this in the name of full employment and economic development.

Roz had bought it in foreclosure shortly after moving to Oresville. For several years she was committed to restoring it to its original beauty with a twenty-first century twist. The kitchen was modernized to the standards of a woman who loved the art of cooking. The rest of the house was a modern, bright, open room concept with walls gone, plumbing replaced, and electricity revamped. The inside was not filled with antiques as one would expect from the appearance of the outside. Fishscale shingles adorned the outside of the structure and were painted in multiple colors that screamed *look at me*. The extraordinary little thirteen hundred square foot house looked happy and radiated comfort, a hearty welcome with a proud Victorian heritage.

The dinner preparations were screaming along as Phoebe struggled into the door with gifts and her contribution to the dinner, several bottles of wine. "Merry Christmas, Roz" and they traded a buss to each other's cheeks. Roz's signature Zydeco music could be heard before the door was opened.

Phoebe dumped the gifts under the blue-themed decorations on Roz's tree and took the wine into the kitchen. Each burner was topped with a pan, bubbling a Cajun or Creole concoction with varying combinations of crawfish, seafood gumbo, and collard greens. The presence of Tabasco Sauce could not be missed. The cornbread in the oven was adding to the ambience, and the incredible aromas were adding to the sensory overload.

Roz grew up east of Lafayette surrounded by the Atchafalaya Swamp and *Looseeann* bayou country. She was not content to live surrounded by water, cypress trees, creepy alligators, and a messed up family life. She liked to say she worked her way through high school selling cosmetic products and magazine subscriptions. At graduation she packed her Cajun culture, Zydeco music, typing skills, and bought a bus ticket for a place with four distinct seasons, no humidity, and nothing at sea level—Colorado fit the vision.

Today she was dressed in black jeans and a blue satin low-cut tunic covered with a black, floor length waiter's apron smeared in droppings from food prep. When she added black stilettos, she was as tall as Phoebe.

Roz appeared to be enjoying her favorite drink, a Sazerac cocktail. This had been the drink of choice since her twenty-first birthday when friend, Mary Henson, introduced her to it. They had met at the cafe where Roz worked upon landing at the bus station in Pikeview, Colorado. Mary was a frequent customer and had discovered this drink when visiting New Orleans. Roz believed it was a more sophisticated drink than the moonshine her Daddy produced back in the swamps of *Looseeann*.

"Let's get a start on the holiday. What can I get y'all, Pheb'?"

Phoebe was practicing her deep breathing techniques to fully embrace the sharp smells percolating in the kitchen. "Anything will do. I have to work tomorrow, so one and done, as we say."

"Well, let's make it count in that case." Roz handed Phoebe a full bottle of wine and a glass. "There's your one and done, Sista." They both laughed. It was a great beginning for friends being together on this special day.

Bill Diamond pulled up in front of the house in a Sheriff's squad car, one of the perks of being the Undersheriff of Green County. The necessity of a Green County car for personal use was an incredible misuse of taxpayer's money but the Sheriff's office justified the expense. The citizens needed the Undersheriff to be quickly available at all hours. It would be a waste of critical time driving to the office before going to a crime scene. The residents would smile and tolerate any idea with a cover story of safety for all dwellers in Green County. Elected officials fully embraced this nuance and used it indiscriminately as the trump card to get whatever they wanted.

Loaded with an assortment of foodstuffs perched on a tray and bags bearing gifts, Bill waddled up to the front door avoiding the patches of old ice and fresh snow. Phoebe met him as he made a grand entrance with his million-dollar smile. Taking the tray of food from his hands, she noticed he was outfitted carefully in dress slacks, tasseled loafers, and a deep blue sweater that matched his eyes. Amazingly enough he also matched the blue theme of Roz's elegant Christmas tree and Roz herself. Phoebe was wondering if she had missed the memo or was something else afoot?

He set the gifts under the tree, slipped out of his top coat and took a nanosecond to check hair and general appearance in the window of the side door. This was so typical. He had been doing these self-inspections since he was young, growing up with Phoebe and Carrie Jean in Salt Lake City. Phoebe seldom noticed this occasional checking unless he did a pregnant pause to perfect the reflection. Then Phoebe and Carrie Jean together would jump on the slightest opportunity to tease him about his manly man appearance, just as they did years ago.

Occasionally one of them would mention to him in a low voice that his incredible blond hair was looking flat. That would send him into a frustrated frenzy in an effort to look for the closest mirror while fumbling to find a comb, a brush, or hair product to get the blond curls *just so*. The teasing did not stop there. Phoebe and Carrie Jean occasionally discussed within earshot a random faux pas such as spinach in a tooth, toilet paper dragging on a shoe, or his fly unzipped. After twenty plus years of friendship, starting in childhood, the trio had carte blanche for any level of harassment.

He had greeted Phoebe with a slight kiss on the check and a quick brotherly hug. To Roz he did a more than friendly bear hug and a deep lingering kiss. Phoebe was surprised by this demonstration and knew this was more than a casual fling between the two of them. *Wonder when this started? Nobody has said word one about what might be going on.*

Tapping Bill on the shoulder, Phoebe interrupted what was going on, "Ah, excuse me. I would suggest you two get a room, but that could actually happen given we're in a house with bedrooms."

They each laughed and stepped apart, looking more than a little flushed.

Bill cleared his throat, "Let's do a bit of business before the party rolls. I need to get caught up. Any news on your dead or worse victim from Wurtz Ditch?"

"Nothin' much. I hear she might have been at the Buns on Sunday."

Roz nodded before a sip of her Sazerac, "Oh yes, I heard about some ruckus there. Rumor has it there was a crazy deal going on between two people last Sunday. The woman told Becky to shut the 'you know what' up. I'd not want to be the one to cross that boundary with the likes of Becky. She's one tough chick."

"Amen to that." Phoebe made the sign of the cross as if to ward off the random spirits that come with acknowledging the truth of the statement.

Bill added to the mix, "I'm thinking we need some credit card information to track this woman over this last week or so. That little talk yesterday in the conference room with the supposed husband was a fiasco."

"I'm curious too, y'all. Thinkin' I might just slip into the office tomorrow and see if anything has come back. I put out some feelers yesterday, but by the time I left the office yesterday, nothing had stirred the pot. Holidays and whatever." With that comment Roz gave a meaningful look at Bill.

Phoebe thought she saw Roz give him a raised eyebrow adding a come hither look on the whatever gesture. "I assume you went through formal channels, right?"

"A lady never tells." With that comment Roz giggled, breaking the ice and giving way to the start of the full-on holiday celebration with work in the rear view mirror.

Just then the front door opened and a rousing, "Merry Christmas" was announced by the arriving guests. Carrie Jean and Brian were coming in, followed by coroner, Doc Jon Watson and his niece, Laurie Watson. Everyone was loaded with gifts, contributions to the dinner and lots of Christmas spirit. Carrie Jean and Brian were reveling in the joy of their new engagement. Jon Watson was happy to spend the afternoon with his niece in the warmth of Roz's lovely home. Roz was delighted to see her friend Laurie.

JOYEUX NOEL

The giant Higgins Homestead was screaming Christmas. For the first time since electric lights were installed, every nook and cranny on the outside of the Edwardian house was beaming into the late afternoon and evening air. From outer space it would have been an honorable mention on the globe. Grandma Connie had the house was completed in 1905 when she was twenty-one years of age.

Constance Higgins, the daughter of Sam and Molly, was living in the family's homestead cabin, in the middle of nowhere. Orphaned at the age of fifteen in 1899 when diphtheria wiped out the family, she moved to the safety of Oresville and the business interests she had inherited.

Being the only heir to her family's Colorado mining wealth, she became the richest female west of the Mississippi. Grandma Higgins, back in Omaha, took over. To assist with Connie's recovery from the loss of her siblings and parents, Grandma decided a trip to Europe was called for—just what the doctor ordered. This would not only broaden the teenager's view of the world beyond mining but also provide an opportunity to teach this child the finer points of life. Her financial interests would be attended to by the family's lawyers. The six-month trip with grandma turned into what would come to be called a Gap Year Plus. More than two years later Connie returned to the States, ready to assume her standing in the community and grow the business interests in Colorado. At seventeen she was already divorced from husband number one.

The Edwardian design for homes was all the rage in London. Connie brought these new building designs back to Colorado. With her worldly ideas and demonstrated promiscuity, she would not be relocating to Nebraska. Grandma Higgins was delighted and the rest of the family relieved. To show their support, they sent the family architect to Oresville and enough workers to create whatever the entitled young woman wanted. The result was a design with lots of windows, wide hallways, large, tall, open rooms, and running hot and cold water. To the shock and awe of the townsfolk, Connie moved the outhouse inside. The gardens in the front were award winning should there ever be a competition. The Connie Higgins house was a focal point for the community and Connie's unspoken bragging point.

The house was completed despite design changes every month or so and now Connie had an operations base. She went to work spending money by investing in local business startups, buying buildings and land in surrounding towns, and ranching in the Arkansas Valley. When prohibition started in January of 1920, she was prepared, having already harvested the ingredients for bootleg liquor. She converted downtown vacant storefronts into small shops with speakeasies tucked away in the back rooms. These establishments in all of the nearby towns provided jobs and goods for the locals, and adult entertainment for those who wished to participate. And, Connie had a marketplace for her bootleg whiskey operation.

When the depression hit in 1929, she employed people to work in her silver mine, The Last Hurrah. Not only did Connie keep her storefronts open, she expanded her work forces in other areas too. Carpenters were put to work building homes for the miners. Building new houses meant plumbers, painters, and bricklayers were gainfully employed. Suppliers of goods were thriving. Connie turned the depression into boom times for Oresville, building a strong following of committed, hard workers. Her creative thinking and generosity were legendary in the Arkansas Valley. If anyone were to ask Connie to what did she owe her success, she cocked her head and answered, "I never hesitated when an opportunity appeared. "Ready, fire, and maybe aim, if it didn't slow me down." She was an explosive business woman. Nothing got in her way.

Connie was a focused business woman. She turned over very few of the business interests to Anne Louise, observing that Anne was more of a social butterfly than a business woman. Grandma saw the potential for success in Augusta and started grooming her to continue the family's track record. The plan she had for Augusta programmed her into the Colorado School of Mines to fast track her into the family businesses. There was no line item for the luxury of holidays, vacations or general time off. Living in the mountains of Colorado was considered to be enough of a vacation. Augusta was laser focused on preparing to take over directly from Grandma Connie. Fast track was an understatement.

Decorating the house for Christmas had never occurred to Augusta until Queennie Lewis came to visit. Augusta lived in the house every winter while her mother and Uncle Q were livin' the dream in France. Now that they had returned and intended to move into the Higgins residence, Augusta was thinking decorating for Christmas would be quite the welcome for dear old mother and Uncle Q. Queennie was busy bringing up her decorations from Pikeview and searching through the hidden areas of the house for the necessary trinkets.

Queennie's idea for every holiday was an easy recipe—lots of friends, food, cocktails, decorations, regardless of the event, and a barbeque grill for summer happenings or a firepit for the winter holidays. Along the way she had announced, "Time for this old house to come into the twenty-first century." With the nod from Augusta, she had rewired the house for music, TV, and internet in each of the six bedrooms, the office, the carriage house, the kitchen, five bathrooms, and all of the common living areas including the front and back porches. Augusta was enjoying the new lifestyle and perspective Queennie brought with her and readily picked up the tab for the equipment. Queennie did the engineering and supplied the labor.

Augusta had grown fond of Queennie and enjoyed her company. Queennie would break free from work and come to Oresville on the weekends. With a flair for orchestrating events, she had offered to come to Oresville and create the Thanksgiving celebration for Augusta and all of their friends. It was an amazing event. Queennie's motorcycle friends roared into Oresville on a bright, sunny, fifty degrees Thanksgiving Day for the one o'clock feast and frivolities. Knowing what they did about her culinary skills, had the weather not been perfect, they would have driven anything with wheels or walked or hitchhiked to attend the event. She went overboard on the food with an easy, nonchalant approach supplemented with plenty of wine and drink throughout the process. Augusta was assigned the task of finding the Sunday Best for serving—

silver that needed polishing and china with just the right crystal.

Setting the table for twenty-three people was Augusta's one and only assignment. The guests were all of various callings in either Oresville or Pikeview, few of them knowing both Queennie and Augusta. Queennie's energy was infectious and an hour into the dinner gathering, everyone was friends or at least friendly and smiling. The talk, laughter, and toasting was accelerated by the music from the speakers in the ceiling. The Higgins Mansion had not seen this much fun in several decades.

Four weeks later, Christmas would be a day of quiet celebration, gift giving, food preparation, and time with close friends and family. This was something that Queennie fully embraced. It would be a much smaller crowd than the Thanksgiving feast, but intimate and comforting with Anne Louise and Quinton finally home.

When Augusta and Queennie met at the memorial service for Old Al they had the instant friendship of *opposites attract*. Queennie was outgoing, spontaneous, and loved being with people. Augusta was serious, business minded, strong willed, and could easily live in a small town where she was a big player. Her life was comfortable at 10-5 through the winters, and she enjoyed the peace and quiet on the mountain top all summer at her mine, The Last Hurrah.

Years ago, when Grandma Connie passed away, Augusta grudgingly dropped out of the Mines and returned home. She was much better suited for the business world than Anne Louise, whose interests were more oriented to Oresville's limited social setting. Although the inherited business interests were run primarily out of Omaha and needed little oversight, Augusta had her own ideas of how to grow the mining, ranching and properties in Colorado. Anne Louise had few ideas to put in place now that Grandma Connie had passed. She needed Augusta to step into the driver's seat for the Oresville businesses and assume her place among the wealthy leaders of Colorado.

For this Christmas season, the outside of the Edwardian was decorated by local high school kids under the supervision of their football coach and Queennie's direction. In exchange, there was a sizable donation made to the team. Enough to guarantee new uniforms and equipment.

Augusta and Queennie declared a tree decorating party the Saturday following Thanksgiving and invited Phoebe and friends for a "drinks and decor" party. A tall, fresh cut spruce was brought into the main parlor, the white lights were draped, and ornaments were applied. Augusta was surprised when Queennie found boxes of hidden decorations in the attic, securely tucked away labeled in Grandma Connie's handwriting. A beautiful star they found topped this handsome creation. Queennie had brought her collection of two hundred or so nutcrackers and they were proudly displayed throughout the common living areas.

Four weeks later, in preparation for Christmas dinner, the dining room table was covered in an antique Irish linen tablecloth with an array of candles in the center. Fresh pine boughs finished the table decoration and the family china, crystal and polished silver was in place for Round One. It was an exquisite sight to behold. The kitchen held the remaining tableware to be used when the guests arrived for Round Two—dessert. It would be a jubilant day for all.

Early afternoon on Christmas Day, the first guests arrived—Mother and Quinton. Anne Louise was a fashion statement to behold. She had on a long sleeved, floor-length gown of silver threads against a red, heavy satin material. Her pure white hair looked brilliant, mimicking the glimmer of the satin threads. Quinton was a handsome guy as always, wearing a grey suit with a red satin shirt open at the neck. His curly hair was grown out to look like a loose-fitting cap adding two full inches to his height. The smile he carried topped whatever he was wearing on any day. Today his style was the exclamation point to Anne Louise's silver.

After welcoming the guests, Queennie stepped back into the kitchen and was mixing the opening cocktail for the four of them. Anne Louise was making a mental note regarding the clothes Augusta was wearing for this holiday. Not nearly as formal as Anne Louise's gown but the black satin pants and red velvet jacket were close enough to "holiday festive" to satisfy her upscale taste as inspired by the French. Queennie was in black leggings and tunic top with just a touch of red from a scarf. Her long light brown hair was beautifully styled into a french braid. Each of them was acceptable in her acquired European opinion and their looks complimented each other. Anne Louise liked to be the one in the room who was dressed to notably stand out, even in her own home.

"Augusta, you've outdone yourself. The house looks beautiful. I cannot remember the last time nor the first time I saw a Christmas tree in here," Anne Louise said a little more than wistfully.

Growing up in Oresville, Anne Louise spent every summer and most holidays with her Grandma Higgins, in Nebraska. It was there she learned the social graces expected of a Higgins child and came to understand the social standing and leadership expected of her in the big city. These skills and preferences did not transfer well to Oresville. With Connie running and growing the businesses in Colorado and Augusta dropping out of the School of Mines to take over when Connie passed, Anne Louise had it easy. Her long-term relationship with Quinton Garrett was the magic formula for livin' large at 10-5 and she was delighted to leave Colorado several years later for the pleasures of Europe.

"Thanks, Mother. Glad you like it. Queennie and I had a ball putting all of this together, with lots of help and drinks. We had a winter barbeque with some friends for the beautification of the tree. Queennie planned it all."

Anne Louise skipped the conversation forward to the dining room setting, "Oh, and look at this magnificent table. You two are amazing."

"Well, I thought it'd be good to make this Christmas a special one. You and Uncle Q are back and it'll be the last Christmas I'll be living here." This comment came out with a caustic ring to it.

Today's opening volley was appropriately stated. Augusta could not contain the bottled-up frustration with her mother.

"Merde (shit). That had not even occurred to me, you know, that you might want to continue staying here. Why didn't you say something? You wait until this special day to drop the guilt bomb on me?"

"Where did you think I'd live when you came back to Oresville?"

"To be frank, Augusta, no idea. I hadn't given it any thought. We planned on staying at Quinton's house until the holidays were over to give you time to decide where you would go. I assumed you had a plan like you usually do."

"That's the problem, Mother. You don't give any consideration to the impact of your choices. You left me here with nary a thought of how that might affect my life."

"Now, now, Augusta, let's sit in the front room for a few minutes and have this out, just the two of us. You've not been happy these last few weeks since we've been back. Quinton can stay in the kitchen with Queennie. She might need some help." Quinton took the hint and gladly left the two of them as they moved into the other room.

Getting settled Anne Louise asked, "Where does one get the name Queennie? Did her mother have high hopes for her?"

Augusta laughed, "Not quite. Her mother named her Martha. Queennie's the nickname her motorcycle friends gave her, cuz she's always ridin' high."

"She's not that tall."

"They did not mean it in that way."

Anne Louise looked confused, "Ah, well, there you have it then," and let it go for bigger questions.

"I think I've just been wrapped up in my own life, Augusta, and have not thought enough about how us living in France would affect you. You're so capable, so talented. I thought getting out of your way would be easier for you and your various husbands. Oops. Sorry, that slipped out."

"Let's not start on my various husbands. That ship has sailed. The elephant in the room is finding a winter place for me, Mother. For once this is not about you."

Anne Louise skipped over the last comment. "You can stay here with Quinton and me. There's plenty of room and we would hardly even see one another. You could do all the cooking and Quinton loves to do dishes."

"That's a negative, Mother. I need my own space and there's Rose to think about. Now I might have added Fido."

"I thought Fido was your dog. Wrong?" Just then Fido heard his name and came racing into the room, sat on his doggy haunches facing them, and dropped a tennis ball at their feet. Someone had tied a Scottish Tartan red plaid scarf around his neck and he was looking cute and hungry. Hanging out with Queennie in the kitchen for a few days, the dog looked to be putting on weight.

"He's in what we call active storage here at the house. I'm just keeping him until Phoebe can sort out what's what with the rightful owner." She picked up the ball and gently tossed it down the long hallway towards the giant Christmas tree.

"Dear, I don't think it's a good idea to throw that ball in our home. He's no lap dog that can easily maneuver. He's actually one of the largest Labrador Retrievers I have ever seen, but he is cute in his own way."

"Yes, Mother." Augusta was impatient with the conversation and mother advising on a dog that is unofficially not even part of the Higgins Household.

"What about Albert's mule, Rose? Is that beast in this active storage too?"

"The jury's still out on her."

"I have already been approached by Onis Adams. As town magistrate, he has rules and regulations to enforce, you know. It isn't all up to you. The animal needs space and the neighbors need peace and quiet."

"The neighbors can mind their own business."

"Now Augusta. You need to think about this. This isn't the Wild West. Having a mule in our yard is not right for the mule. Do you think Rose likes living in town? And the yard needs daily maintenance with the, ya know, droppings."

Augusta had to laugh at the delicate choice of words from her Mother. For the first time she realized that her Mother might be right. "Let me worry about Rose. I'll fix this before you and Uncle Q move back in."

"You could temporarily move up to the Higgins family homestead. Rose and Fido would love it at the cabin. It's a cozy place to be in the wintertime."

"We should probably talk about the cabin. It's a lot of work to maintain, now that Albert has passed. Finding good help to work on it has been impossible. I hated to take the necessary step, but it was inevitable and long overdue in my latest assessment. A lost cause."

Anne Louise heard what she wanted to hear and interrupted Augusta. With a light clap of her hands she declared, "Good. Then that's settled. I'll let the postmaster know she can back off too. Where did they dig up that one? She's difficult to deal with, a real delicieuse (delicious), as we would say in France. As soon as I told her my name and expectations, she stomped away, and left me talking to myself."

"You're calling her delicious? I never learned to speak French, but I don't think that's the right word for the witch that she is."

227

"That's what I meant, a real delicieuse," she said with a heavy French accent to stress her practiced, albeit confused use of the language.

Just then Quinton came into the room. Having overheard the conversation he corrected Anne Louise, saying to Augusta, "She meant to use the term chienne (bitch)."

With a heavy frost to her voice, Anne Louise turned her back to him saying, "Thank you, Dear Quinton, as was my intention. I misspoke myself." She continued the conversation ignoring his presence in the room. "Regardless, Sweetie, you're my daughter. How can I make this up to you?"

"Let's stop right here and talk about the cabin."

Quinton was half-heartedly listening and teasing Fido with the ball who was prancing in anticipation. With a quick snap of the wrist, he winged it down the hallway. Fido raced in hot pursuit, all fours flying with full out concentration on the toy. He nearly caught up to it, but proceeding too fast to stop at the tree.

The following events took place in slow motion.

They all turned to watch as the ball took a hefty bounce and lodged in the long branches of the elegantly decorated tree. Anne Louise could feel what was coming and was the first to quack out a guttural, "Stop." This was followed by shocked looks of disbelief from Augusta and Quinton. The three of them watched, their faces turning in unison from the dog, to the ball lodged in the tree, and back to Fido.

Queennie exited the kitchen headed for the group. She tossed a kitchen towel over her shoulder and cracked her knuckles. She rounded the corner in time to see poor Fido crash into the giant tree. It seemed to be suspended in air, ignoring gravity, and thinking about where to go as if a tree could decide. In total confusion, she froze, her mouth dropped to a perfect 'O' and watched the tree begin a slight sway with a tip to the south, quickly picking up speed. The tinsel was swinging, and an occasional ball could be heard busting on the floor. The multiple strings of lights started flickering and popping.

Closest to the pine, Queennie lunged, trying to avoid Fido who was struggling to get out from under the action, crying and yelping. She took charge and started directing traffic. "Stand back everyone. I'll handle this." Her long arms sprawled into the limbs grasping for the trunk to stop the fall.

Quinton was galloping down the hallway, yelling, "I'm sorry, I'm sorry!"

Just as Queennie gripped the trunk with one hand, Quinton reached the tree in time to help stabilize and set it upright, but the damage was done. Lights were intermittently perking with a sizzling noise, broken Christmas decorations were scattered on the floor, and the tinsel was in sad-looking knots.

With all the fun and excitement, Fido began his "cute mode" of romping around the tree barking hysterically. He lunged his mouth into the evergreen branches, bit the tennis ball, and raced back to Augusta and Anne Louise, dropping it to the floor for another toss. Anticipation radiated from the tip of his nose to the point of his tail.

Anne Louise and Augusta were in shock, sitting in disbelief with what was happening. As they recapped the details later, they agreed staying out of the action was the right thing to do.

The noise was over and everyone was incredulously staring at the space where the tall tree had proudly stood. The silence was broken when the music from overhead started the tune, "Rockin' Around the Yuletide Tree" by some church choir whose director had rewritten it to be a holiday hymn in two-four time. The classic three-part harmony felt like a funeral dirge. How appropriate.

Queennie took a deep breath and on the exhale seized the moment announcing, "Well, that went well. Cocktails in the kitchen everyone. Now."

Anne Louise and Augusta looked at each other in disbelief. At Queennie's direction, they rose in unison, not saying a word, and with heavy steps moved toward the kitchen. The cabin discussion was not going to continue under the present circumstances. Fido raced in front of them, ball in mouth.

The order of business called for serious adult beverages.

BAYOU BOUNTY

Rosalind Marie Beaudreau had outdone herself with the holiday dinner. With an emphasis on her heritage, straight out of the Louisiana bayous, Roz had set up a spread the likes of which had never been seen by these guests.

Then there was the unfinished conversation she had with Phoebe before everyone arrived. When Bill came into the house and unloaded gifts, food, and booze he stepped into the bathroom. Phoebe in a lowered voice asked Roz what the deal was with Bill, "Roz, I notice something more than friends with benefits between you and Bill. What's the spiel? Your next mistake approaching on the romance road or some fun holiday action?"

Roz looked surprised and stepped back. *Am I that obvious with Bill?* With a two second pause she replied, "Too soon to tell, but so far things are looking good for these cold winter months at 10-5." She added a quick wink to end the conversation as Bill came into the room.

Phoebe let it ride, but wondered when she could say the same thing about her and Bart. He's in her thoughts more these days and she was looking forward to his visit for the New Year's Eve party.

The nagging details around Ellis and Mickey Walker popped into her thoughts again and she blurted, "How does a relationship survive domestic violence?"

The question caught Bill up short, "Come on, Phoebe, this is a party. Where'd that come from?"

The first to venture an answer to Phoebe's question was Roz, "I saw this lots growing up in my family. Dismal outlook, constant financial woes, and alcohol the answer to 'What do we do now?' Why do ya think I left the first day following graduation? I owe it all to Avon, typing skills, and magazine subscriptions."

"Avon?" Bill gave Roz a surprised look. He clearly had never heard her talk about her home life. "Well, okay. Let's put this on hold for today. Can we talk in the office tomorrow? It's Saturday, but I'll sacrifice a day off to put this together. Are ya thinking he tried to off her?"

"I don't know why she was up there. I'm thinking about her off the road and left for dead or worse. Now I

234

know way too much about her relationship with Mickey to let it ride."

They both looked at her, "What'd you find out?"

"Well, it turns out their marriage includes domestic abuse."

"Mickey is part of this? I never would have guessed that of him."

"No, not Mickey." Phoebe looked at Roz, "She's the aggressor. He got a restraining order against her. They lived in Greenstone or she still does. A little birdie told me."

Roz ventured, "Ponytail Guy is the birdie? Y'all can tell us."

"I didn't exactly go through formal channels for this, so birdie it is."

She moved on and was hoping for some kind of flash insight on the subject. "That's part of this whole narrative. We're not comfortable talking about domestic abuse and it's as old as civilization."

Roz started to say something but their thoughts were conveniently side tracked when the other guests arrived all at once. Bill nodded to Phoebe, "For sure we'll talk tomorrow morning at the office."

Carrie Jean, Brian, Jon and his niece, Laurie Watson, brought the energy needed for the merriment to begin. After sharing warm greetings with the newcomers, Roz turned to Bill. "Oh, by the way, Bill, would you mind playing bartender for all of us today? Brian could use a break, I'm sure."

"I'd love to. Now you all will see how we mix drinks at 10-5 without recipes or correct ingredients."

Laughing, the guests attacked the appetizers with gusto as the cocktails were mixed, swirled, and drizzled with the shaker in constant motion.

Phoebe was leaning over the range, fanning the smells towards her face, "Roz, how did you manage to get this all done? Everything looks and smells delicious." Phoebe attempted to shelve their previous conversation and begin anew.

Roz took the hint, "I love to do this. It reminds me of my childhood in the bayou. The table might not have been so fancy, but the food was incredible.

The small group moved around the crowded kitchen enjoying their drinks, admiring the array of pots and pans emitting incredibly delicious aromas. At four in the afternoon, they moved to the dining table. Of particular note, was the centerpiece. It was intended to be a compliment to the food and the Cajun themed dinner. Roz had clipped some greenery from neighboring pines and added fishnet stocking strips from an old Halloween costume. Fake shrimp, fishing lures, and a token alligator were carefully placed to create the holiday decoration. It was a true *Looseeann'* Christmas display.

After sharing their compliments on the decor, Roz and Bill brought the food to the table. The blessing was put through the wringer by a verbose Carrie Jean. The usual hot air flowed as a stream of consciousness and all of those gathered at the table nodded in agreement as the past year was recapped. She went into a lengthy statement of praise for friends who are like family and those seated with her shouted a hearty, "Hear! Hear!"

Then the prayer wandered over to the past year's clients of Jon, the Green County Coroner, who was nodding in agreement. He was also the only mortician in the county or double duty as he liked to say. He went so far as to make the sign of the cross in respect for those who had passed his way for services.

Carrie Jean was channeling her years in the schools of Salt Lake City. The blessing moved on to cover Principal Laurie Watson's elementary students who under her firm leadership would move into their teens. These years would be hard fought with braces, pimples, and raging hormones. At the end of middle school, they would move into high school only to continue the anguish of the teen years, but with new teachers and fresh driver's licenses.

Lastly, she moved onto the subject of fresh starts for people at the table, namely the New Year and as an example of "new" the wedding for her and Brian. Stopping for a deep breath was a mistake. Everyone took the opportunity to effectively end the diatribe and yelled a rousing, "Amen," with a gusto eliminating any chance of the blessing saga to continue. This served as a full stop. Everyone took a moment to agree with her words, breathe in the incredible aromas, and feast their eyes on the bounty before them. Finally, they could eat.

Doc joined in the conversation, "Glad I didn't eat all of those interesting boiled peanuts and your spicy chicken dip. I don't want to miss a helping or two of everything on the table."

"Well, let's pass these dishes around," directed Roz. "Bill, you start with the chicken and sausage gumbo. Doc, you grab the dirty rice. The shrimp and grits are in front of you, Pheb', so you start with that. I'll pass the jambalaya and CJ, you pass the collards. Oh, here's the cornbread comin' round."

"Looks like we've got everything covered," said Phoebe. "This is a wonderful meal with fabulous friends. Thanks for the wonderful spread, Roz."

As the friends tasted, smacked, and slurped, each person in turn offered up a toast to the particular dish they admired, thanking Roz for all she had done to make this a festive meal for these guests. It was starting to sound like a canonization of Roz. She blushed with the compliments and sat smiling, sipping her watered-down white wine spritzer.

"What? No Sazerac for you? That's not like our Roz." called out Carrie Jean.

"Nah, just trying to pace myself. It's been a long week and it's far from being over."

They all ate until they could eat no more, and sat back comfortably to give their stomachs a chance to rest.

Bill offered the final toast to Roz, "This was unbelievably good. You certainly brought your Cajun heritage to Oresville today. Let's drink a final toast to my Roz."

What did I just hear? My Roz? Oh, I have to get to the bottom of this story, the sooner the better. Phoebe was in shock.

"I loved every minute of it and I got to share this special day with very special people." She looked at Bill.

He was already looking at her with a look in his eyes Phoebe hadn't seen before.

"And now, the pièce de résistance. Everyone stay put. I'll be right back." Roz hurried to the kitchen.

Entering the small pantry past the refrigerator, she carefully lifted the covered cake plate off the shelf and carried it to the table. "Ta da!"

As she took off the cover everyone did a sharp intake. Roz had created the most beautiful cake they had ever seen.

"This is a Doberge Cake. A Cajun specialty, born in New Orleans and named after a Hungarian Dobos Torte. There are six layers of white cake, alternatively filled with lemon and chocolate pudding. On top of a thin layer of buttercream icing there's a white fondant shell. The Christmas decorations of miniature blue and silver Christmas balls and fresh greens are an added touch. We'll be takin' this cake over to Augusta's."

Once the oohs and aahs were done, the cake was packed for the short ride to Augusta's. The table was cleared and the comradery continued as each person found a task, making short work of the clean-up. Once all was in good order, everyone retired to the cozy living room and the gifts were passed around, along with after-dinner cognac with a grasshopper on the side.

The gift exchange was predictable as these people had been together for many years. Roz, Phoebe, and Carrie Jean always exchanged hardcover books from a best seller list. This year with Laurie Watson joining them they included her in the book category. Doc Watson, Laurie's uncle, provided a box of chocolates for the ladies and cigars with electronic, rechargeable lighters for the guys. The lighters were the latest gizmo on the market to catch his attention.

As the guest from Greenstone, Laurie Watson brought an assortment of refrigerator magnets. Each was handmade by the artisans at the city's art center, individually numbered and signed. She also shared the narrative of how naming the town in the 1800s had led to a heated argument by the town fathers. The Longfellow poem "Hiawatha" was popular and many of the residents thought naming the town Gitche Gumee would be an accurate, unique name for the twenty plus effervescent mineral springs in the area. Somehow, logic won out and Greenstone became the middle of the road in the argument.

Roz presented the men with special black satin sleeve garters. The men looked at them and checked the name on the wrapping. They were thinking these were for the ladies in the room. Roz had to explain that they were to hold up their sleeves to stay out of the way regardless of bartending or performing mortician duties. For Bill Diamond a sleeve in the way was not much of a concern. She gave him a gift subscription to Sock of the Month, a beautifully designed sock issued each month for the best dressed among us. He was delighted.

Bill Diamond had Green County Sheriff ball caps fresh off the press for everyone. If not employed by the Sheriff the cap read Honorary Member and included a toy old west Sheriff's badge and handcuffs. For Roz he had added two additional gifts. The first was a beautiful necklace of her birthstone. Before he could stop her from opening the last gift, she ripped off the wrapping and held up fur lined handcuffs. There was a half-beat of silence as the group tried to absorb the gift. Once they realized what Roz had in her hands there was some wild clapping and whistles, fueled by too much Cognac. For these friends, it was truly a day to remember.

Phoebe could not keep her mind totally on the celebration. Her mind wandered to Bart, wondering how his day was going. She decided a quick call to him on her way to Augusta's would help settle the question.

And she still had the mystery of the accident to deal with, a young woman in a hospital bed, and a disinterested husband. She still did not know the husband's involvement following their big blow up at the Buns.

Suddenly it occurred to her, the big question she was avoiding. Would she be this interested if the driver were a guy and the abuser in the marriage? Typically, this was the case sixty to seventy percent of the time. A much smaller percentage of spousal abuse occurred when the female was the abuser and if the players were under fifty years old, only fifteen percent would show the male as the victim. Seldom would she run across a case of a young man being abused by his wife. This is why she was so interested in trying to understand what gives with the Mickey and Ellis relationship.

Her mind whirred along, trying to keep things in order. *Nothing you can do about any of that right now girlfriend. Live in the moment and enjoy yourself. Tomorrow will take care of itself.*

The cuckoo clock in the living room let loose with an irritating tweet announcing time to move over to Augusta's for dessert. Roz announced, "Time to up the action into phase two of this party. Let's move out."

The group quickly gathered the castoff wrappings and ribbons, stuffing the debris into the trash. Bundled into coats, scarves and gloves, they tried to manage the slippery walkway with controlled sliding, careful balancing, and lots of cuss words to invoke the powers that be for safe passage to their respective cars.

Just as the exit began from the front door, Roz cooed in a honeyed Cajun accent, "Oh, Bill, would you help me with the cake please?"

"Would love to. Please proceed, folks. I'll drive Roz and the cake over. We'll be right behind you."

Phoebe wondered, yet again, *what is going on with those two?*

As soon as they entered the kitchen, out of sight of the others, Bill leaned her against the sink, slipped his arms around her, and looked into her eyes.

"You did a terrific job here today, Honey. I don't know how you do the magic, but it sure does work. Thank you."

"You're welcome. Hope y'all liked the gift."

"I do and I hope you like the necklace. Can we try out the special cuffs later?"

"Absolutely! How about we come back here after dessert and I'll model both the cuffs and the necklace. A special dessert just for you."

His mind fixated on the image her suggestion invoked.

"And the necklace is beautiful. Just so ya know for future reference, my motto is 'Gold Always Fits' so when in doubt, go gold." Roz added a serious look to permanently lock in the plan for later in the evening.

"Thanks for helping with everything. Now let's saddle up the cake, big boy, and see about growing the party at Augusta's. I saw Queennie at the marketplace buying tons of food. She's a great occasional addition to the neighborhood and I think her positive view on life is rubbing off on Augusta."

Bill was beaming at the thoughts of action later tonight. He got back on track with Roz's thinking, "How so?"

"Like a year ago, Augusta would never have volunteered to take in a dog or actually have a friend like Queennie or decorate her huge house or invite us all there for this dessert gathering. They're opposites and best of friends since Old Al passed."

"She probably felt guilty about killing off Old Al with her arsenic-laced special tea."

"Oh, Bill. You don't know that," and she playfully pushed his shoulder.

"Well, it probably hurried the end for him along with the fact that he was called Old Al because he was, well, old. Not to mention, drinking fresh water from streams where he was panning for gold. Yuk."

Bill's eyes drifted to his image reflected in the window above the sink. It was dark outside at six o'clock on this cold, still, winter night, so their reflection was clear. Together, comfortable, the special link between them was so real to him. Suddenly he spotted a chunk of hair out of place. From years of practice, his hand slipped into a shirt pocket, whipped out a little comb, and corrected the errant wedge. He did a quick check of his profile from each side. Roz smiled at the perfected view.

They grabbed the Doberge cake and departed for Augusta's.

ROUND TWO

The group of seven arrived at the Higgins house with a grand entrance. "Merry Christmas everyone" chimed the group. "Let the desserts begin." Anne Louise met the group at the door and announced, "Au revoir (goodbye)! Come in!"

Quinton corrected with a great smile, "Bienvenue chez nous (welcome to our house) is what we meant, not goodbye, right Annie?"

Ignoring his comment, Anne Louise added, "Quinton, dear, I designate you as the person in charge of coats, hats, gloves, and handbags." And she helped everyone with their outerwear, purposely throwing each piece at Quinton's waiting arms.

After a confusing time trying to organize the pile without handing out coat check tags like a professional, he tossed everything into a glorious pile on the front sitting room sofa and announced, "Fend for yourselves." None of this was a problem for the arrivees. They had consumed a sufficient amount of Christmas cheer to not care what happened to their coats.

Anne Louise made a mental note to get the handling of guest's belongings under control. This was one more thing needing attention if they were to assume a rightful place in Oresville society. She announced, "Right this way people, and please disregard the frightful array of trimmings on our tree."

This comment brought the little entourage to a standstill at the base of the towering tree. Several remarks were muttered, all of them a variation of, "What the hell happened to the tree?" Since early afternoon the tree was securely anchored to the wall in two spots, just in case there would be another mishap. The busted balls, lights, and twisted tinsel had been swept up and the majestic tree looked slightly less elegant. Fido was dancing around vying for attention. Despite the disaster that had just occurred, his playfulness was not diminished. Thankfully, the toy ball had been readily hidden.

Without belaboring the stop at the tree, Augusta announced that the family's newest pet, Fido, had a mishap and the humans were to blame this time. They began sharing stories of their dogs, cats, and hamsters in a previous life and Fido's misadventure was quickly forgiven. They moved on to the dining room where the table was set for desserts and the strong smell of fresh ground coffee permeated the air. The gifts from under the tree had been moved to become the centerpiece of the dining table and the guests added their gifts to the pile.

TuTu and Jorge were helping to get everyone seated and comfortable around the huge table. Queennie took the drink orders. She and TuTu hustled into the kitchen to prepare the potions. The Drink of the Day was declared to be a hybrid Jolly Old Fashioned, consisting of bourbon, Campari, angostura bitters, muddled orange slices and some cherry juice to make it a holiday red in color. Coffee was served as an aperitif to the start of desserts.

Phoebe remembered her promise to TuTu regarding the name of the driver left for dead or worse. She caught up to her in the kitchen and asked for a few minutes before the round of drinks were served. They stepped into the library. "TuTu, I wanted to get back to you on the accident we were talking about at your place."

"I've got a bad feeling about what you're going to tell me. Did she die?"

"No, she's recovering in a hospital in Pikeview. I'm looking for information on her. I don't know what she was doing up there by herself. It's unusual and I was thinking you might have some thoughts on it."

"Sure, if I can help. Do you have a name?"
"Ellis Walker."

TuTu seemed shocked when she heard the name. Her face took on an emotional surge. "Oh no, she was at my workshop all weekend. That's what she was doing here in Oresville. The session ended on Sunday morning before noon. This happened on Tuesday?"

"Tuesday is when we found her. I haven't figured out when it happened, but I have a journal or diary of hers. The notes in it talk about the snow storm and being stuck off the road. I would say it happened on Sunday."

"I need to go to her. This is my fault for not following up."

"How can this be your fault? I plan to track down her husband tomorrow and get more information. I think they were at the Buns on Sunday afternoon. It did not go well."

"I hate to leave Augusta's party, but Jorge and I had better pack up and get down to the Pikeview hospital."

Everyone was getting settled in the dining room. Anne Louise started telling them about the demise of the Christmas tree, when the phone rang. Augusta excused herself and joined TuTu and Phoebe in the library to answer it. Hank Williams was calling to thank her for the generous presents she had sent for everyone in the Klingfus family.

Queennie and Augusta never had children to buy for and shopping for the Klingfus family turned into an unbelievable event for the two of them. They expanded the shopping to take in a non-profit on the west side of Pikeview and another one in Oresville. Augusta had the financial bandwidth to make a difference and Queennie knew how to shop.

When Augusta met Hank, he had dropped out of school in Greenstone. He refashioned his status into what he called an Early Gap Year, thinking it would be easy to get a job. The application process pretty much put the kibosh to that spin. Augusta had taken Hank under her wing after Old Al, Hank's mining mentor, died. She told him if he quit this idea of a gap year and went back home to finish high school, there would be a job waiting for him at her mine, The Last.

This young man brought out a dormant maternal instinct in Augusta and she saw his potential. With her encouragement and some financing, which she could well afford, she had visions of Hank at the Colorado School of Mines, living his dream of prospecting for gold and adding to her dream as well.

"Augusta, your gifts made this a wonderful Christmas for me and my family," gushed Hank. Let me put my brother and sisters on the phone to thank you for their gifts. While you talk to them, I'll check on the dinner I'm cooking for us."

At home with Hank there was a younger brother, George Jonas, and two younger sisters, Dolly and Loretta. The children were named after country western artists by the creative Mom. Dad went with any of her ideas as long as he did not have to get involved beyond fulfilling his role as the sperm donor. Mom and Dad lived in their own dream world.

"You're welcome, Hank. You cooked dinner?"

"Yup. Good thing I'm back at home or Christmas dinner might have been hot dogs." He let out a sarcastic laugh.

"Well, you're quite the caretaker for your family. I hope you know that I'm proud of you."

"Thanks Augusta. Here's George Jonas. I'll get back on after the kids are done."

While the conversations with the Klingflus children proceeded, Augusta made a personal decision. She would take up Queennie's offer of a place to live near Greenstone for the winter. With that move, she could keep a close eye on the kid and perhaps give some direction to his sketchy family. Currently the information she received on Hank was thoroughly massaged at the community table in the back room of Mo's diner. Bart would pick up the fresh gossip about the Klingfus family and deliver it to Phoebe who would pass it along to Augusta.

Hank returned to the phone when his siblings completed their talks with Augusta. "Hank, I just made a decision. I am going to spend the rest of this winter in Pikeview, living with a friend of mine. It'll give me some time to spend with you and hopefully meet your family."

"That's great, Augusta. Keep me posted and thanks again for everything. Merry Christmas."

"Merry Christmas to you and your family. Bye for now."

TuTu and Phoebe were in the room overhearing this announcement and the direction of their talk was quickly put to the side.

Augusta hung up the phone and looked at them. A gasp of silence and then the questions popped. Yes, she was moving to Pikeview to live with Queennie temporarily until she could build a place to live in Oresville away from Anne Louise and Quinton.

The three of them walked into the dining room and Augusta looked at her family and friends gathered around the table—laughing, talking, and listening. The evening was in full motion. The streaming music from the ceiling speakers started into yet another holiday tune that had been heard so many times it no longer registered as music. TuTu tapped a spoon on the nearest glass. The room became quiet and they all turned to the ladies standing at the head of the table.

"Augusta has something she wants us all to know, don't you Augusta?" TuTu turned to her, and then nodded to Phoebe, who nodded back.

Looking at Queennie, Augusta lowered her voice, "I would like very much to take you up on your offer of living with you in Pikeview. I'll spend the winter there closer to the kid. He's next door in Greenstone and I think I can help him get through his senior year. Maybe help him to a solid start in life."

The whole room started asking questions and Queennie got up from the table and went to Augusta. She gave her a big old bear hug and they both had teary eyes. The room immediately got louder with questions, questions, and more questions. The New Year promised to bring even more changes—a wedding, new shifts for work schedules, and now a person living at something lower than 10-5 for the first time in forty years.

Augusta's mother smiled wide, clapped her hands, and exclaimed, "Merde!"

CHICKENS HOME TO ROOST

Saturday morning started cold, windy and generally "winter miserable." The perfect morning to stay in bed and ignore the world. Except Phoebe couldn't stop thinking of Bart and reached over and picked up the phone. Much better plan than lying in bed debating about getting up and doing all the usual morning rituals of cleaning, scrubbing, organizing even though nothing demanded attention. She was thinking mornings were the perfect time to work on changing her ways. The slight register on her self-diagnosed compulsive scale might be fading as her call rang through. She heard Bart's deep voice and snuggled under the blankets.

"Hi there. How's life this morning"

"Good. You'll be jealous. I'm still in bed. How ya doing?"

"Fine. Things are pretty quiet here after the big non-event holiday yesterday. Fortunately, we didn't have any major crime events and I'm hoping for another quiet day. How was your dinner and dessert at your friends' homes?"

Phoebe was thinking he sounded a bit down after a holiday by his lonesome. "Very nice. The food was great and so was the company. Sure wish you could have joined us."

"Me too. I have to admit it was an empty Christmas, but then someone has to work the shifts on holidays, me being single and all."

"Yea, I know the drill. So sorry you had to be alone on Christmas Day. Not fun, but how generous to volunteer to cover for the married officers. Even though I was technically on duty, here I can be on call instead of cruising the neighborhoods alone in the patrol car."

Sounding a bit tired and maybe a little down on spirit, he responded, "Nice. I sure am looking forward to New Year's Eve. It'll be great to have a break and get out of Dodge. I'm to arrive in Oresville at the Club at 9:00 p.m. Right?"

"Yes. I'm looking forward to seeing you too. It's a special evening at the Club, so we have an excuse to dress up in our party best. Make sure you have your dancin' shoes on. There will be a DJ, and snacks ala Roz. She's our local party plannin' gal. I'm excited for you to meet all the people I've been telling you about for months."

"In the meanwhile, I've got information on Ellis Walker. TuTu and Jorge Tavarez are retired ministers. She runs counseling sessions for women in troubled relationships. Each week there's sessions via the phone, but once a month for a weekend the clients meet in Oresville. When I told her it was Ellis in the Wurtz Ditch accident, she and Jorge left Augusta's home and rushed to the Pikeview hospital. Tutu knows that Ellis doesn't have any family and she and Mickey are separated."

Bart added, "He would not go to see her because he has a restraining order against her."

"Right. That relationship is likely over."

Phoebe went on to tell Bart she knew that TuTu, a Good Samaritan, would be supportive of Ellis. "TuTu's a real asset to the town, helping in many different ways. She owns a local washateria, where folks can get their clothes clean, and get a hot meal with some kind of beverage. Payment is optional—'Cleanliness is next to Godliness' is the Tavarez mantra.

"Turns out, Ellis was here last weekend for TuTu's monthly workshop. Appears that when the meetings were over on Sunday, she stopped at the Buns and met up with Mickey who was on his lunch break. That did not go well. As a new hire for the county, he works the weekends, so Bill and I plan to track him down this morning and get his side of the events of last Sunday. I'm hoping to tie up the loose ends and see if we can lay this baby to bed sooner than later."

"Well, good luck with all that. Let me know if there is any way I can help you. Oh, gotta go. Other line is ringing. Thanks for your call, Phoebe. Always good to hear your voice."

With a soft voice she replied, "You too. Bye for now, Bart." Listening to the silence, she gently hit the disconnect key.

She stayed in bed another half hour, enjoying the luxury of reminiscing about yesterday's Christmas festivities and not cleaning the already clean floors. Dinner at Roz's was delicious and the evening at Augusta's turned out to be a great time for all.

Carrie Jean told the friends over dessert, "As a result of Roz's Cajun dinner, we'll be speakin' with a *Looseeann* accent by the time it travels through our digestive tract." The group agreed and this set off an exercise in accent-practicing similar to speaking in tongues. Carrie Jean always thought in terms of e-Blast! headlines. She could see it now, "Cajun Accent Explosion."

For the dessert party, Roz's spectacular Doberge literally "took the cake." It was almost too beautiful to cut, but in short order all were served. Strong chicory coffee was served on the side. It's naturally caffeine free, perfect for this nighttime dessert. Queennie had thought of everything.

She livened up the gathering with a dice game for door prizes, Winner Takes a Gift. The dice were hot and the action was furious. Everyone had won one of the three door prize gifts at least twice before it was lost to the next winning shake. The hard stop came at the forty-five-minute mark.

"You lucky winners of a door prize are now on the hook for next year's hosting of the Christmas Desserts and Drinks," chuckled Queennie. There were shouts of "no fair" and "oh, yeah?" that greeted the news, all done in good humor, for sure. It looked like Phoebe, Bill and Quinton were on the hook for next year's Christmas event.

TuTu and Jorge had excused themselves following Augusta's announcement with nothing being said as to where they were going. Sudden departures were not uncommon with these two ministers when a member of the flock called, they answered. Phoebe had asked TuTu to contact her as soon as she had spoken with Ellis.

As Phoebe threw off her blankets, the phone rang. It was TuTu calling with an update. "Hi, TuTu. How's it goin'?"

"Good. I'm here with Ellis and she's doing well. Looks like the docs have her blood sugar under control and there appears to be no lingering effects from the cold or the slight concussion from a bump to the noggin. She'll be released today. I'll get her to the house in Greenstone."

"That's great. I'm anxious to talk with her. First, I'm going to the office to meet Bill. We'll locate Mickey, who is supposed to be working this morning and interview him. How about I get that done and give you a call back?"

"That'll be fine. Ellis appears to have had a major change of heart as a result of this experience. I'll tell you all about it when I hear from you. Good luck with Mickey."

"Thanks."

Enough hanging out this morning, girlfriend. Get a move on.

She hustled down the hallway to the kitchen, hit the button on her coffee pot, which, of course, was already set up, and meandered back down the hall to take her morning shower. Once done, dressed and ready for the day, she returned to the kitchen to enjoy her favorite—a hot cup of French Roast straight up. She paired her coffee with an English muffin, butter and jam, eaten in record time. Then tidied up but skipped the usual morning ritual of cleaning the trailer for a change.

She was looking forward to the meeting with Bill at the Sheriff's office. Roz would be there to look for credit card receipts created on the trail of the Ellis Walker weekend. It would take a half hour at the most but Roz promised Bill she would not charge the department overtime. As Acting Sheriff, Bill wanted to be sure nothing impacted Sheriff Joe's budget on his watch.

The day following Christmas was a big letdown and the town was taking a sigh of relief. Phoebe was not working patrol today, since she was assigned to detective status.

As Phoebe was driving into town, she couldn't help but wonder about Roz and Bill. *They sure were acting pretty cozy yesterday. Perhaps my detective skills could be practiced on these two and I can find out what those fur-lined handcuffs were all about.* A provocative smile followed this visual.

Bill's squad car was in the parking lot in the back of the Sheriff's building. *Great, he's here so we can get this show on the road right away. Roz should be here any time now.*

She parked and entered the building via the rear door. The conference room was on her left and she turned in to leave her coat, gloves and scarf, only to be surprised to see Bill and Roz holding hands at the table. *What in the world is going on here? Where is her car? Did they come together? Oh my. This is serious. Will I be the only single one next year?*

"Good morning. How's everyone this morning after our day of revelry?"

"Great," they mumbled. "Good mornin' back at y'all."

"I've got to get to the front desk and start my credit card search for you, Pheb'. It shouldn't take long." Roz jumped from her seat and started out the door. *Is that a blush I see on Roz's perfect olive skin,* mused Phoebe.

"OK, I'll be back here." Turning to Bill, Phoebe said, "Have you located Mickey yet?"

"Yes, I saw him and asked him to join us. He had one job to complete and said he'd be right over. How about a cup of coffee while we wait? Roz got it started."

"Great."

When Bill returned with the coffee, Phoebe tried to prep him for the talk, "Let's get this interview organized, Bill. Where shall we begin?"

Just then she heard footsteps in the hallway. Roz called out, "Company on its way."

"Well, let's just keep this open ended and see where it goes," Bill offered with a shrug.

Phoebe lowered her voice and quickly added, "I want to be more direct. We need information on his part in this, if anything."

Phoebe literally bit her tongue and grimaced. *I can't believe how loosey goosey Bill can be when information is critical. We need to know Mickey's part. Are we dealing with a crime or bad driving with poor judgement?*

Mickey entered the conference room, cup of coffee in hand. Dressed in work clothes, he looked neat enough, but tired.

"Hi. I got here as soon as I could. I have about twenty minutes and then I need to get back to the job."

"No problem. Let's get started. I'd like to record this if you're okay with it. Saves me time taking notes." She added a friendly smile that did not reach her eyes and moved the pad of paper for note-taking to the side.

"That's fine. I don't have much to say, but ask away."

She turned on the recording device. "Today is December 26th. In the room are Deputy Korneal, Undersheriff Diamond, and Mickey Walker."

Bill cleared his throat, "That would be Acting Sheriff Diamond until Joe gets back."

Phoebe gave him *the look* that said a thousand things without speaking.

She looked back to Mickey, "Please tell us about your relationship with Ellis and the events of last weekend."

Bill added, "Yup. Just start talking. We'll interrupt if something isn't clear."

"When I was here on Wednesday, I wasn't willing to talk about my personal life. I'm a new employee and I wanted to get off to a good start, not carry my rocky marriage into this job. Now I realize that you need to know what's goin' on between Ellis and me."

Phoebe agreed, "Exactly."

"She is aggressive, even abusive toward me when she gets angry. The last straw was when she rear-ended my truck with her car a few months ago. I think she would have killed me in the heat of the moment. That's when I placed a restraining order against her and moved to Oresville. I'm done."

"Is this the same vehicle she was driving last Sunday?"

"Yes, she commutes to a great job in Denver and her car was out of commission from the accident. My final act as husband was to give her the truck. I got the car fixed for myself. She still hasn't fixed it, but it's not my problem anymore. I haven't taken the time to transfer the title to her name yet."

Mickey was slowly flipping his cell phone cover open and closed with a click. Click. Open. Click. Closed. Click . . . Phoebe was watching this, thinking, *Here's that tell again. He's nervous about something.* She made a note to herself. *It's probably this uncomfortable subject of spousal abuse. Am I rationalizing here?*

"Ellis has anger management problems and I'd say it's getting worse. Even though she's been working with Reverend Tavarez to get control, it's not helping from what I can see. I moved to Oresville to try to get a perspective on starting over and let her work out whatever, minus me as her victim. Then I ran into her at Becky's Buns Up last Sunday. I work weekends and was finishing lunch when she came in. She saw me at a table, came right over, sat down, and started yelling 'What are you doing here? Are you following me?' Of course, I wasn't following her. I didn't even know she was in town."

With head down he took a shaky breath and appeared to be on the verge of tears. Phoebe hated interviews like this. Its gut wrenching for the toughest of law enforcement officers to witness the personal side of someone's life. The cell phone action had picked up speed. She was thinking, *He's nervous about something in this story. Perhaps just talking about the subject.*

Phoebe waited a heartbeat then urged him to continue, "What happened next."

"Well, the owner of the Buns asked us to leave because she was making such a disturbance. So, we went out to the sidewalk. Ellis said she was going for a ride up the mountain to clear her anger. I told her not to go up there, but Ellis does what Ellis wants to do, especially when she's out of control. She was driving toward Azure Lakes with my dog, Fido. I followed her just in case anything happened. She's not so good at driving the switchbacks on dirt-packed mountain roads."

Now Phoebe noticed he had added a bouncing foot to the cell phone action. She made another note.

Bill cut in and took the whole interview off track, "There's snow up there now."

Phoebe wondered if Bill had forgotten the weather timeline from last weekend.

Mickey looked at Bill and stopped shaking his foot, "Not on Sunday, it was just a dirt road. It hasn't snowed all winter. So far there's no skiing this winter, right?"

"I hear ya, brother. I'm waiting to go out when it gets deep enough to not ruin my skis on the rocks. At this rate it'll be March." Bill and Mickey shared a chuckle over agreement.

Mickey added, "Pay the price of a lift ticket for the opportunity to ruin skis?" They had more chuckles.

Phoebe was pissed and was thinking. *Shut up, Bill! What's skiing got to do with Ellis? I've got to get this interview back on track.*

Ignoring their ski talk Phoebe jumped in, "Alrighty then. So you followed her up the road?"

"Oh, yes I did. I followed her up the mountain a bit, but the car I'm driving now is not cut out for that kind of road. It's more of a trail than a road, but whatever. When she realized I was behind her, she sped up. Not good. So, I gave up and at the first chance, turned around, and went back to town. I figured she'd just park at a trailhead, settle down, and Fido would help. I went back to work and put my marriage in the rear view mirror. We don't call each other, so I didn't miss her. The first I realized she might be in trouble was when you and the Sheriff mentioned the red truck when you were talking in the parking lot Tuesday morning."

He was again shaking his foot and snapping the phone cover—open click, open click. Phoebe was sitting at the end of the table watching for these nuances. *Something is not solid in his story.* She made herself another note.

"So, Mickey, where do you stand with Ellis now?" Bill was having a hard time grasping this relationship even though he was divorced with two teenage kids and a spiteful wife in Denver.

"Believe it or not, after all we've been through in our short relationship, I still love her. Ellis is a good person with a big problem. I haven't been able to help her and it seems her sessions with the Reverend haven't helped either. If I had any hope, Sunday at the bakery ended it. So, where do we stand? I don't know." He lowered his eyes and sighed. "I hope she gets some help."

Phoebe prompted him back to the Sunday description. "You turned around and then what did you do?"

"Went back to work and I was late. I had to work late to make it up."

"What time did you get back to work?"

"Hum, about one fifteen or so. I was a half hour late getting back so I made up the time at the end of the shift."

"OK, no worries. I was just wondering that's all. Thanks for taking the time to help us understand what happened, Mickey. I think we're done here, right Bill?"

Bill nodded, "Maybe we can go skiing sometime?"

"Sure thing," and Mickey left to return to work.

What? Phoebe rolled her eyes, *This is a non-event for Bill.* She couldn't help but feel sorry for Mickey, *but why so nervous?* He seemed sincere and clearly in his mind the marriage had no future. She had Ellis' view from what had been written in the diary, but no mention of Sunday's events. With a better picture of the weekend, she was anxious to call TuTu. It was beginning to feel like a drive to Greenstone would be needed to wrap up this investigation.

Best to keep conclusions out of the picture. Check Mickey's schedule for last Sunday. Get the facts girlfriend. Get the facts.

269

After Mickey left the conference room, Bill looked at Phoebe, raised his hands and blurted, "A woman driver, poor judgement, mountain roads—write it up, case closed. Need anything else from me?"

"No. I'm good for now, Bill. I'll follow up on Mickey's schedule last Sunday and get on the phone with TuTu. I expect I will need to go to the Pikeview Hospital to talk with Ellis. Getting her side of the accident will put this whole mess together. I'll let you know what I find out."

"Whatever," shrugged Bill. "I think a trip to Pikeview would be a waste, but will leave that to you."

"Hey, is Roz still out there? I need those credit card reports."

On the pretext of getting the credit report, Bill quietly asked if she was ready to go home. His mind was still on those fur-lined cuffs.

"Here they are, Pheb'." Roz yelled. She added at a lower level, "I'm ready to go when you are, Bill." She gave him a mischievous smile accompanied with a long, lingering pause, then sashayed down the hall to the conference room. "Here ya go. Hope it helps. I'm leaving now unless you need something else."

"Nope, I'm good. Enjoy your weekend."

"You bet we will," smiled Roz as Bill joined her to exit the building.

Something serious here. I need to get Roz alone and interrogate her. It's time I knew the scoop before CJ gets it.

Phoebe chuckled to herself. This is turning out to be quite the end of the year with all sorts of loose ends to be settled.

Getting her thoughts together, Phoebe phoned TuTu. "Hey, I just finished my interview with Mickey. What's happening with Ellis?"

"Well, we have some good news here. Ellis is doing well and the doctors have released her. I'll be taking her home in about an hour."

"That's great. I'd like to drive down and talk with Ellis at her house or I could request some interview space at the local PD in Greenstone. What d'ya think?"

"I'm thinking the house would be more comfortable."

"Does she remember her drive up the road?"

"I think so. She admitted to me it was her own fault. This is a big step in the right direction for this young woman. I'm amazed at her transformation. If you leave now, you'll be here in something like two hours or so. Right?"

"That's close enough for government work. Text me the address and I'm out the door. Thanks, TuTu." She could hear her laugh at the government comment.

Phoebe was ready to hear Ellis' narrative and wrap up a solid week. Driving across the South Park Basin, she was thinking a call to Beautiful Man would be a surprise move and they could have an early dinner together. She decided to wait on the call to Bart until she talked with Ellis. At that point she could determine if the case is closed or she would be investigating a crime. If necessary, she could get Acting Sheriff Bill Diamond to arrest Mickey. Plan for the worst and hope for the best.

FLIP SIDE

The ride to Greenstone was a relief for Phoebe. It gave her time to mull over the information from Becky and Mickey about the Sunday events. Now she could open her mind to listen to Ellis. *Mickey was sincere today but I'm not ruling out the possibility he forced Ellis off the road and left her for dead or worse. A "claim of no knowledge" from a sincere hubby has been heard many times, thank you very much. Please let this conversation with Ellis put the whole case in perspective.*

Driving to Greenstone, Phoebe took a deep breath and turned on the radio. She had thought through her plan and now relaxation was in order. She sang along, off key to one of her favorite country western tunes, *Three Sides to*

Every Story. How appropriate. The tightness of the week drained off and she was ready for this interview, whatever it brought to the table.

TuTu's car was in Ellis' driveway. Phoebe pulled in behind it, and followed the brick walkway to the front entrance of the Craftsman bungalow. There was a beautiful wreath hanging on the wooden door, a cheerful sign of the season. As she knocked on the door, she could hear footsteps hurrying her way.

The door opened and TuTu gave her a warm hug and a smile.

"Glad you're here. How was the drive?"

"Easy peasy, TuTu. No problem."

"Well, c'mon in then and join us in the living room."

Phoebe looked over the small, cozy front room. The small side chairs were covered in chintz, the sofa a soft green. Walls were painted a mellow yellow and all five windows had white lace curtains. Nothing expensive, but all put together it was a pleasant, comfortable room. Sitting on the sofa was Ellis, looking pale and fragile.

"Hi Ellis. I'm Phoebe Korneal, Deputy Sheriff of Green County. So glad to see you. I was the deputy at the recovery location on Tuesday."

"Good to meet you too. TuTu has told me about you. I'm looking forward to talking with you."

TuTu interjected. "How about some coffee and cookies? We stopped at the store on the way home to grab a few essentials. The cupboards were bare."

"Sounds good, thank you. It's a long drive." Phoebe was a bit hungry and those cookies sounded perfect.

"Have a seat, Phoebe. I understand you'd like to ask me a few questions about last weekend."

"Yes, I'd like you to tell me what happened. Mickey and I have talked and it's important that your details be heard."

Ellis took a deep breath, pulled her shoulders back as if to gain strength and looked directly at Phoebe.

"This is difficult for me, but it's time I got my life, my relationships and my anger under control. As you may know by now, I've been in the counseling sessions with TuTu, either by phone or at monthly meetings in Oresville. This past weekend was the onsite meeting and I was there from Friday evening until lunchtime on Sunday. The group has been together most of the year. We help each other deal with out-of-control relationships. We work well together and the Reverend is great.

"Well, I shared, once again, how angry I become when things don't go my way. And, more often than not, Mickey is the target of my anger. But he's been gone for several months now, so the people I work with are the closest. It could be something simple like misspelling a word on a report. Somehow, it triggers my anger and I'm out of control. This has become troublesome. That's what happened last Sunday at lunch time. I like to go to Becky's Buns Up for a quick lunch before I check out of the hotel. There was Mickey. My first thought was he was following me, which set me off, and despite just coming from the monthly retreat, I confronted him, immediately out of control. The owner asked us to leave. Once outside, I realized I should step back from the mess I was creating.

"I took his dog and told him I was going to take a drive on a mountain road to calm down. He said I shouldn't go. There's lots of switchbacks. Of course, I didn't listen. I sped out of town and up a dirt road toward Slide Lake. Driving up the road, I saw Mickey following me. That really pissed me off, so I tromped on the gas pedal and the engine responded. Next time I looked back, he was gone, but I didn't slow down. I entered a hairpin turn and felt the loss of traction. In a flash I was shooting off the road. The next thing I remember is waking up in a cave."

"In a cave?"

"It felt like a cave. Actually, I was in the cab and it was totally covered in a blanket of white. My head was pounding with a big bump. It was freezing cold and I was woozy. I realized I didn't have my insulin. Thank goodness for Fido. He kept me warm and awake as much as possible. I must have passed out again at some point, because the next thing I remember, I woke up in the hospital."

"Lucky the snowmobile club riders found you. This was a very close call, Ellis."

"I know. It's changed me in ways I find hard to believe. Sitting in the front seat and close to death, I had a vision. I could see how my behavior is so destructive to me and everyone around me, especially Mickey. The cause of my anger has deeper roots and I'm using him as the nearest target. I've made a commitment to address the root cause or causes and use tools, maybe medicine to control my anger. I'm committed to making my marriage work if Mickey will have me back. Despite it all, I love him and want him as my husband."

"Wow, Ellis. Looks like something good will come of this not so good event. I need to ask, how was it you went off the road?"

"Traveling too fast, poor judgement, and out of control anger. The tires don't have good tread, it was the perfect storm. This was all my fault. My mistakes, my bad behavior, my foolishness. I almost lost my life, for what? This disaster has changed me."

"So where was Mickey in all this?"

"I don't know. Last time I looked in the rear view mirror, he was not there. I just know if he had seen me go off the road, he would have helped me, despite my temper tantrum."

"I'm glad to hear what you just said. Your side of the accident puts everything into perspective. I'll close this case, knowing you were not the victim of a crime, but the victim of your own bad choices. I hope you and Mickey can find a way to heal your relationship."

"Thank you. I'm praying we can, especially with the Reverend's help."

Sitting quietly and listening to Ellis, TuTu nodded in agreement, "That's what I'm here for Ellis. You can call on me for the support you need on this journey."

TuTu had heard this a hundred times before and knew the odds for success were slim to none, but she didn't voice her experience.

Once Phoebe said her goodbyes to TuTu and Ellis, she drove over to La Cocina, the Mexican restaurant that she and Bart had gone to when they first met. Sitting in the parking lot, ready for a surprise visit to Beautiful Man, she called him.

"Hi, Phoebe. I was just thinking about you, wondering how your case is going."

You're thinking about me? Yikes. Getting over her surprise she calmly answered, "I believe it's close to being all tied up. I've interviewed the players and I have one more thing to validate. If that checks out, then it was an accident, pure and simple, with dire consequences. When I get back to Oresville tonight, I'll swing into the office and take care of it."

"Don't tell me you're in Greenstone interviewing Ellis Walker?"

"In fact, I'm sitting in the parking lot of La Cocina."

"Darn it anyway. You don't get to Greenstone very often and I hate that I'm out of town."

"Well, I didn't mean to bother you. I was hoping we could meet for a quick dinner before I drove back to Oresville. Oh well, always a next time." Phoebe tried to chuckle over her disappointment.

"I left at lunchtime to spend time with my brother and his family. They came out to Breckinridge to ski. We don't get together much, so I'm glad he invited me. Who can refuse a day or so of vacation in the mountains, right? We're doing some skiing and trying to reconnect."

"Cool. I wondered if you knew how to ski."

"I do. Cross country is the first choice for me if I can't get to Howelsen Hill for jumping."

Phoebe sighed with the thought of skiing cross country. That is a lot of work and not easy like downhill blue runs or the fast Double Diamonds. Then add to the mix, ski jumping? *No way!*

Living in Colorado, skiing can mutate into a DNA factor. The first skiing in North America was founded in Colorado by Norwegian immigrant Carl Howelsen in 1914. Carl would be amazed today to see his Howelsen Hill surrounded by the town of Steamboat Springs. The Hill has helped to produce nearly ninety Olympians over the years and is designated a Pioneer Ski Resort.

Bart returned to her comment about the restaurant, "La Cocina, right? Every time I go there now, I think of our first lunch together."

Every time he goes to La Cocina? "That's a nice thought, Bart. Thanks for sharing it. I'm looking forward to your visit next weekend."

"You can be sure I'll be there. It'll be fun to celebrate the ending to a great year."

With the letdown of Bart not in Greenstone, Phoebe was feeling cynical, "As years go, this one's over."

"I was thinking of our meeting in August."

"Oh, yeah. Right. That too." She decided to take a risk and added in a hesitant voice, "This New Year's Eve could kick off a great year for us."

"I think it's promising. Let's hope it doesn't include another trip to the ER."

"Me too. What's left of the little mark on my lip, actually reminds me of our first real date."

"That was quite the evening." They smiled in silence at the memory.

Bart continued, "I have two officers on the force who promised they would take my shift. I've done them a few favors over the years."

"All right. Enjoy your time with the family and I'll see you in a few days."

"You bet, Phoebe. Take good care."

As she disconnected the call, Phoebe had a strange feeling, like she really missed him. *Be careful, girlfriend.*

Don't let your guard down. Try not to get your hopes up too high. The fall isn't a pretty one.

The early dinner hour was quiet in the restaurant. A perfect time to think about Beautiful Man and where this relationship might be going. *Could this actually work?*

The two-hour drive back to Oresville was uneventful for a Saturday evening. As Phoebe drove across the flat expanse of South Park, she could imagine the ghost of Sam Hartsel who grew his homestead from one hundred sixty acres to ten thousand in the late 1800s.

The early darkness at this time of the year was nearly daylight with the full moon. The air was clear and crisp at eighty-nine hundred feet in elevation, surrounded by the Rockies. Tonight she could have used a sextant to navigate with the blanket of countless stars illuminating the night sky. Sam's town of Hartsel is the geographic center of Colorado and the nearby South Platte River makes the entire basin all about fishing and hunting. There is even a buffalo herd. The straight, flat, two-lane highway enabled faster driving, allowing vacationers and residents an easy reach for a full day in a thriving mountain community like Breckenridge.

Back at Oresville, the Sheriff's office was quiet and her focus was finding Mickey's timecard. She ran a copy of it for the case file and noted the stamps on it covered these last two weeks of the year. Last Sunday he had clocked in at one twenty-five p.m. after the lunch break. This was the last piece of the puzzle for the case and it all fit. Ellis and

Mickey were each telling the truth. Ellis was the victim of her own anger and reckless behavior. Phoebe wondered what was going to happen to their marriage and reminded herself, *Stay in your lane. Or as Roz would remind me, not your circus, Pheb'.*

Phoebe completed the paperwork on the case. There would not be a ticket issued. Technically the incident occurred on National Forest Land, no one died, and the Walkers were responsible for their own decisions and now the pricey helicopter ride and hospital stay. The search and rescue work is free, but donations are the lifeblood of this amazing group of dedicated, round the clock volunteers. Tomorrow's schedule put her back on patrol coming in at two p.m. on Sunday.

It had been a busy week, including the holiday festivities. She was relieved to wrap up this case. Everything was filed and she sent an email for Bill's review. This called for a quiet evening with a small glass of white wine to relax. Feeling a bit melancholy, she turned on her 'go to' playlist—the sad one. *Looks like my single friends are moving away from being single. Will I be the last single woman standing?* On the brighter side, her thoughts turned to New Year's Eve and the anticipated visit from Bart. *Which nightgown should I wear? The black one or the red one Bart gave me? Decisions, decisions.*

Memories of the festivities at the Higgins Mansion were tucked away and the house bespoke a relieved quietness after a month plus of planning, decorating, gathering, eating, talking, and laughing. In return for a hefty contribution to the high school, the proud, dispirited tree would be disassembled and carried away by the Oresville Triple Trio Blasters who were also reprogramming the music system for non-holiday hits. The outdoor lighting would be taken down by the Oresville Rockers football team and carefully labeled for next year. Queennie and Augusta had the crystal and china ready to be stored. The Home Economic Classes, along with the Future Wives of America Club (both known as the Life Skills Groups in big cities) were busy labeling the dinnerware boxes, numbering items, and smoking cigarettes behind the carriage house whenever they could sneak a break. In return for their hard work, they had earned a contribution from the Higgins Family for new garbage disposals in each of the Home Economics classrooms, critically needed by those who were not kitchen-gifted and talented.

Augusta asked Anne Louise and Uncle Q to come over for a Saturday Happy Hour drink and chat. Turns out Queennie had to make a quick trip to Pikeview to check on her radiator business and Augusta thought this would be the perfect time for Dear Old Mother to hear about the cabin and for them to discuss what was left of their Mother-Daughter relationship.

"Bonjour (hello), Mademoiselle," said Anne Louise as she came in the front door. Quinton just rolled his eyes, let his face fall into a grimace, and slapped his forehead.

"I think that would be Bonsour, Madame. I left Mademoiselle by the wayside in my teens," smirked Augusta.

"What may I fix for you each to drink? This is a happy hour and we should treat it as such."

Uncle Q promptly announced, "Don't even think about it Augusta. I'll be glad to mix the drinks. How about Wanton Whiskey Sours all around?"

"Merde," Anne Louise said as she sat down on the sofa with a flourish and a smile. With that word, Quinton raised his hands slightly and indicated 'I give up.'

She patted the area next to her on the leather sofa, "Come sit down with me, Augusta, and tell me what's on your mind."

"Well, Mother, we started this discussion on Christmas day, but were interrupted by the tree topple event."

"That cute, but large dog. What an interesting addition to our home," she was smiling with a suggestion of angst.

"I'm not clear on his status as an addition. He's 'active storage' until something better comes along. In other words, he's not permanent. Temporary. Let's move along, shall we?"

"Certainly, Dear."

"There's some news about the family cabin I need to share with you."

"What do you mean?"

"I've been trying to tell you, Mother, I was overwhelmed. You and Uncle Q took off to Europe, free as birds, and I was left here handling the businesses, this house, and everything else around here. I felt totally alone with you gone and then I lost Al last August. He and I were best friends for years and his loss hit me hard. You remember that he took care of the family cabin during the winter in return for a place to live?"

"He was essentially homeless, Dear, but we Higgins take care of those who are worthy, don't we?"

"Yes, we do, plus anyone else who can use a helping hand or two. But that's not what we're here to discuss. During Phoebe's investigation of his death, it was discovered that both wells at the cabin were contaminated with arsenic. The well at the Last was also bad. It was all so mind boggling and with Al gone, everything fell to me. Too much. No way could I add all this to my already vast responsibilities. So, thinking you and Uncle Q were never coming back to Oresville, I lightened my load and burned down the cabin. Mother, I was so angry with you and that old place was a royal pain in le cul, if you'll pardon my French, Mother."

"A what? Oh, never mind. Augusta. I had no idea. The cabin's no big deal. In fact, I'm at a loss as to where it was located. Who wants to live in a log hut, anyway? Ha, not me and I'm sure Quinton Dear would agree. But, Augusta, I never realized how you felt."

"You know you always appear to be in control, cool and confident. It never occurred to me that you would miss us, or need us for that matter. I'm sorry to have caused you this worry. You're my daughter and I love you, regardless of the number of times you get married, burn down the family homestead, or park a disgusting old, angry mule in my front yard. I can't imagine what the neighbors think. I guess I just never let you know how special you are to me. It's important for us to have some fun before I kick the bucket, ya know?"

Augusta was listening raptly, for the first time in a long time, and valued what her mother was saying. She did not feel the spite she had felt when she set the cabin on fire. "I have to tell you I'm sorry for what I did, but at the time it seemed right. I'm sorry."

"Augusta, don't mention it. Lots of good memories with that cabin. My Mom, Connie, loved to tell the story about how someone designed a fireplace for the outhouse. Remember that one? Then it got out of hand and within a month the fireplace malfunctioned and burned the outhouse to the ground." Both of them had a good laugh with the thought of what that outhouse looked like.

"Thanks, Mother. You'll probably outlive all of us and I'm glad you're back. I want us to spend time together, but I need my own space. Living here with you two isn't going to work. My short-term plan is to spend the winter in Pikeview with Queennie. It'll give me time to figure out a winter place for me in Oresville."

"Well, Augusta," gushed Anne Louise. "I've the best thought. We own lots of property here in town and there's so much renovation going on with the Hysterical Society money finally rolling in."

"Mom, we're trying to play nice and call it by the proper name of Historical Society Fund. Lots of people are pulling together to tap the funds for the Main Street Project. Just saying', you might need to keep that in mind."

"Hysterical or Historical. Tomato - Tomoto. The same thing, so get over it. Perhaps we could take two of the apartments in one of the buildings on Main Street, or choose one that could have the entire top level converted into a home for you? We'd custom design it just for you. You'd have a place for the winter and the Last for the summers. It'd be easy to take care of, conveniently located on the main drag, and we could have fun designing together. You know how I love a decorating challenge. What do you think? Is it a plan?"

"Sounds like a winner. Especially with you at the helm. Looks like we'll be having an exciting new year."

Just then, Uncle Q, the master of discretion, entered the room with a tray of whiskey sours and light appetizers. "Well, lovely ladies, I hope I'm not disturbing anything."

"Not at all. Augusta and I had a lovely chat and now we're planning a wonderful new place for Augusta to live."

"Excellent, Annie. You always do well when you have a project to control in addition to everything else within a hundred miles."

They all laughed, lifted their drinks and Uncle Q toasted, "To us, together for an exciting new year."

"Here, here," chorused the women, and they each took a gulp, relishing their new found appreciation for one another—maybe.

NEW YEAR'S EVE

New Year's Eve finally arrived and the festivities were in full swing at the Club. The gang was all there, happy to be enjoying each other's company and they all felt the anticipation of a promising New Year. Roz, having decorated the hall for Christmas, had little to do to change it up for New Year's Eve. She had located a mirrored Disco ball to hang from the ceiling above the dance floor and set out hats and noisemakers. Everyone was in a party mood. Families were gathering in the dining room and the barroom was full with all the regulars, sharing the local town news.

Phoebe had driven over to the Club a few minutes early. She wanted Roz to give her the once over, making sure her tight black dress was fitting just right, her hair was falling perfectly over her shoulders and her high heels were the right match.

"What do you think, Roz? Is everything alright? I'm as nervous as a cat on a hot tin roof. Do you think Bart will like the way I look?"

"Oh Pheb', you look fantastic. Your black dress fits perfectly and that new push-up bra is doing its magic. Your hair's gorgeous. I know you can't wear it down for work, but those chestnut waves flowing over your shoulders are beautiful. There's no way he'll be able to resist you tonight. I can't wait to see this Ponytail Guy. If he looks as good as his voice sounds, he'll be a sight for sore eyes. After all the years I've known you, this is the only one you have shown any interest in. He must be special. I want it all to work out for you, Phoebe-girl. You deserve a good guy in your life."

"Thanks, Roz. You sure know how to make a girl feel good. How about we find CJ and toast to the evening."

The regulars at the bar were pleasantly surprised to see a sexy Phoebe exit the kitchen and walk toward them. A couple of cat calls for fun and a few wows were heard. Everyone gestured a high five.

Phoebe waved back and twirled around to present the full view. Brian saw them coming and set up three glasses of white wine. Roz nodded to Brian and started a short chuckle, "Better make mine water and add a twist for effect."

"What? Water? What's up with you Roz, a rough week?" teased CJ.

"Well, Girlfriends, I don't think I'll be fitting into this dress much longer, if you get the picture."

Phoebe hesitated while the comment exploded in her brain. With an astonished, lowered voice, "Wait, Roz, are you saying what I think you're saying?"

"Y'all, that's what I'm sayin'."

Phoebe let go with a shocked and surprised laugh.

CJ jumped in with a bewildered, "Who we talkin' about? Did I miss a headline?"

She looked at Roz and then back at Phoebe, whose mouth was open, trying unsuccessfully to make a comment. She glanced at Brian for clarification but he was at the other end of the bar and missed the Roz bulletin. "Hey, please repeat," CJ begged as she lifted her drink to her lips.

To help CJ get it straight, Roz leaned over towards her ear, "I'm pregnant and this is not a news flash, please, Sweetie." Caught totally off her guard, Carrie Jean sprayed the sip of her cocktail out her nose, started dabbing her nose with a bar napkin, and could not take her eyes off of Roz.

As Brian had walked back toward the girls, the front door opened and he took an educated guess, "Phoebe, I think Prince Charming has arrived."

Everyone at the bar turned toward the door. A collective gasp went out with the vision in the doorway.

Phoebe swiveled around and tried to contain herself. There was Beautiful Man, more beautiful than ever.

He was decked out in black and was a sight to behold—black jeans, black tooled leather cowboy boots and a black shirt, with white mother-of-pearl studs. His belt buckle was silver, fitting perfectly above his slim hips and accented his wide shoulders. Shiny black hair was pulled back in a short ponytail and those ocean blue eyes were shining like a lighthouse beacon. *Oh my.*

Gawking at him like a teenage girl, she realized he was looking for her. *Get a grip girl. You look like an idiot. Go get him.* She pulled herself together and walked over to him, grinning like a Cheshire cat. He smiled broadly back at her as she approached.

The lineup at the bar was trying not to be so obvious in their staring.

When Phoebe reached him, he gently leaned into her and placed a quick kiss on her cheek. *Not only does he look fantastic, he smells good, too.* She let out an excited titter.

"Phoebe. Hope I'm not late. And, wow, you look beautiful."

"Thank-you, kind sir. You aren't late and you look pretty darn good yourself. So glad you're here to ring in the New Year with me."

"No place else I'd rather be, Phoebe." He gently took her arm and they walked toward the group at the bar. The friends were like magpies on a telephone line, watching the couple coming their way.

"Everyone, I'd like you to meet Bart Masterson. Bart, this is CJ and Brian, newly engaged, Augusta, Queennie, and coming our way is Roz, your co-conspirator, with Bill Diamond, Oresville's Undersheriff. And walking over to us is Sheriff Joe Jackson and his lovely wife, Mary Margaret."

Augusta, dressed to the nines as usual, was sitting on a barstool next to her new BFF, Queennie, who, instead of wearing her leathers tonight, wore a long-sleeved lace blouse with stylish black slacks. Augusta nodded to Mary Margaret and smiled at Joe saying, "You'll be happy to know that I've found a place for Al's mule, Rose. She'll live out her twilight years at the Higgins ranch out in the valley. You can take that issue off your plate as an end of the year gift from me to you." She let out a laugh and tapped his back to seal the deal.

Joe gave her *the look* and grumbled, "It's about time. Happy New Year."

Augusta looked to her friend for approval. Queennie leaned over and said, "You've made the right decision for Rose and everyone else—neighbors, your mom, and the looney postmaster, Lyla Stoker."

"Thanks, Queennie. You helped me with this one," and Augusta gave her a slight nod of appreciation. Opps, the little bubble popped into her brain and those damn pickle jars of Old Al's gold appeared. *Well, I'll save that fix for another day.*

There were many hellos and handshakes and a bit of small talk as everyone was assessing Ponytail Guy. After all, he was on a date with 'their Phoebe' and had to pass muster. There would be private discussions when the time was right, everyone sharing their opinion.

Phoebe noticed that Mickey Walker was sitting at the bar with the county office receptionist, Suzanne. Did she over hear him say something about dumping his soon to be ex-wife? Suzanne seemed to like what she heard and snuggled up to his arm giving him a long, lingering look as they each laughed. He did not appear to be the shy, level-headed guy she had pegged him as. Phoebe tucked a suspicion away to be watched another day.

Onis Adams and his wife were sitting at a table next to the bar with their friends. Onis approached Sheriff Joe, snapped a spoon against a wine glass to get everyone's attention and announced, "News for you, Joe, after way too many years of being your only town cop aka magistrate, my lovely wife and I decided it's time to follow the sun. I'll retire on our fiftieth wedding anniversary, February 14th, next year." He was smiling broadly with the fun news and those gathered in the bar, started to applaud for them both.

Bart had always wanted to live in the mountains and this might be his chance, with the added bonus of being closer to Phoebe. *Do I understand correctly? There'll be an opening for a cop here in Oresville? What's a magistrate? I'll check this out. It could be an opportunity.*

Augusta's Mom and Uncle Q had just come in and were moving toward the bar. For the first time in years, Augusta was happy to see them. Queennie hopped off her bar stool and lined up tables for everyone to sit together this final night of the year.

Roz had hired a DJ to keep the music playing. Anyone could make a request, and if he had no requests, he created his own. The current tune that just started was a Texas Two-Step. Bill Diamond and Roz hit the dance floor first and they looked stunning. As he spun her around her raven hair flew in the air, the skirt of her emerald green dress twirled around her knees, and they moved gracefully to the music as if they had danced together all their lives. Roz was a true Cajun beauty, dark eyes, golden skin and long shiny raven hair. Bill looked very handsome in his crisp new boot-leg jeans and western shirt. They made a handsome couple. Now we know, this wasn't their first dance.

Bart took her hand and led her to the dance floor. "Let's dance."

"I would love to."

With that, Bart slipped his arm around her back, held her right hand up and easily slipped into the rhythm of the music. *Amazing, he is handsome, nice, fun, and he can dance too. Oh, Lordy.*

The night flew by, with lots of dancing, drinking, laughing, chatting and a kiss or two on the sly. The witching hour was upon them. Everyone gathered on the dance floor with a plastic glass of champagne in their hands. As the DJ kept track of the clock, Augusta made a toast.

"To each and every one of us, may this New Year bring peace, joy, and happiness. Let's bring back wonderful stories to share next year. Cheers."

The DJ declared the New Year had begun. Everyone sang out, "Amen" and took a sip. Bart turned to Phoebe and ever so carefully, kissed her lips. Shivers went up and down her spine and she enjoyed what was happening for the first time in years. *Could this be real? This man is incredible and he doesn't even know it.*

"Happy New Year, Phoebe. I am so glad to be here and not just on a phone call."

"And back at you, Bart. I'm glad to be spending this evening with you, too," and they shared an embrace.

There were many well wishes shared around the room and folks started to drift toward their respective homes. Bart looked at Phoebe and nodded. "Shall we go to your place? Perhaps a nightcap?"

"Sounds perfect. Let's just say our goodbyes and we can graciously depart."

Whew boy, thought Phoebe as she climbed into her truck. *It's been a long time since I've enjoyed someone's company like I'm enjoying Bart's. It was a great evening, but now he's following me to my place and I'm feeling nervous. What's he expecting—what am I expecting? Oh, what the hell, just enjoy, even though on our first date we took a trip to the ER and I ended up with 3 stitches in my lip.* She smiled at the thought.

Suddenly she remembered the red and black negligees and her angst increased tenfold. *I did not take the tags off! And they're both hanging on the bedroom closet door. Am I going to look too anxious, or like a newbie, or worse?*

Carefully pulling into her driveway, Phoebe made sure there was enough room for Bart to pull in behind her. Taking a deep breath, she stepped out into the crunchy cold night and looked up at the dome of the Milky Way. The full moon was just past and the stars carried the promise of a fresh start.

"Right this way, Bart, Let's get out of this freezing cold."

"I'm right with you on that."

After unlocking the door to her small place, Phoebe stood back and swept her arm across her front. "Please, entree vous (welcome), Officer Batty." she announced, trying desperately to keep her jitters from showing.

"Why, thank you, Mademoiselle. I believe I will." With a deep bow, Bart took the two steps up to the doorway and entered Phoebe's rented single-wide.

Looking around slowly, he took in the neat, immaculate living room and kitchen. "Great place," he said as she closed the door against the cold night.

"Thanks. It's served me well these past years. Please, take off your jacket and make yourself comfortable.

How about that nightcap?" *Or maybe more than just a nightcap. It has been so long since I've been with a guy. I'm not sure I remember what to do or how to act. Do I wear the red negligee he gave me or the drop-dead-gorgeous black number? I'm making myself a nervous wreck. Just let nature take its course—what will be, will be.*

"What would you like, Bart? I've got beer, wine, or some scotch."

"What are you having, Phoebe?"

"A glass of wine will be good."

"Then make it two," Bart agreed.

Phoebe was in the kitchen, opening a bottle of Menage A Trois Gold Chardonnay, and getting two wine glasses from her impeccably organized cabinets. *What next—sit in the kitchen, cozy up on the sofa, how about another kiss? We shared a couple tonight and wow.*

Please, Lord, don't let me make a fool of myself tonight. She had to laugh at herself with the plea for divine intervention.

"Can I help you with that wine, Phoebe?" Bart asked as he stood at the breakfast bar between the kitchen and living room.

"No thanks. This is pretty easy. Sure was a fun evening, don't you think?"

"For sure. I enjoyed meeting your friends, but I especially enjoyed spending the evening with you." Bart was hoping that she felt the same way about him, but he wasn't quite sure. *She's a special woman. Please don't let me mess this up.*

Just as Phoebe popped the cork on the wine bottle, Bart reached over the counter and seeing her iPad, he tapped the play icon. The first song started, Patsy Cline's, "I Fall to Pieces."

"Oh no, Bart. That's the playlist I listen to when I am feeling sorry for myself. Lots of sad songs by Patsy Cline and Dolly Parton. Was having one of those days over this holiday week. Let me turn it off."

Phoebe felt somewhat exposed and carefully reached over to tap a new playlist. *Now he must think I'm a sappy, pathetic little girl, thinking about myself. Why didn't I remember to change it?* At the same time, Bart stepped around the breakfast bar and slowly put his hands on her shoulders. Looking straight into those fascinating amber eyes, he said, "It's a new year Phoebe. How about we create a new playlist? One for just you and me? Let's start with, 'Just the Way You Are.' You know, that song by Bruno Mars?"

"I'm not familiar with it."

"Well, let me pull it up on my phone's playlist. How about one more dance?"

Bart reached out to her and she leaned into his chest. He wrapped her tight with his long, strong arms. She hadn't felt this good in a long time. "Yes, Bart, a new playlist would be perfect," she whispered, and returned the hug.

THE LAST SLIDE

Perhaps the wine can wait for another day.

THE BEGINNING!

THE BEGINNING!

THE BEGINNING!

ACKNOWLEDGMENTS

First and foremost, we want to extend our appreciation to the local law enforcement men and women of Chaffee and Lake counties in Colorado, and Pima county in Arizona, whose flexibility and diligence with the citizens in their areas make livin' large in these areas comfortable, interesting, and safe.

We also want to acknowledge the dedicated volunteers of search and rescue organizations in Colorado. These brave people have the tough job of responding to the dire circumstances of residents and visitors who enjoy living and playing in the great outdoors. Kurt Miller, thank you for sharing your experience for use in this story. These volunteer organizations deserve the praise they seldom get.

Donations to continue their training and work are greatly appreciated.

Thanks to Mark Gabardi for sharing his snowmobiling experience of finding a car buried in the snow in the dead of winter. This was the genesis of our story.

We have come to the realization that every day is a new learning curve, just when we thought we were old enough to know it all. To this point, we wholeheartedly thank our friends and families who have supported us through the re-learning of the literary use of the English language and the use and application of family names and antidotes.

We thank our husbands for their loving support and perpetual patience. You helped to keep our heads on straight, pulled us back from the ledge as needed, and vetted Phoebe's adventures in life and law enforcement. We love you and thank you for maintaining a sense of humor through thick and thin as we created this second book in the planned trilogy. Did we tell you there is another book coming after this one? What a ride, eh?

We want to publicly acknowledge Nancy Taylor for her expertise in creative thinking with designing the marketing, maps, and icons. Virtual hugs going to a special sister, Deb Cornell (pronounced Cor-Nell), who has come to be the first reader for the storyline. Her early insights, praise, and encouragement gave us strength to continue and the vision to grow this story. A special hug going out to

ACKNOWLEDGMENTS

Becky Sloboda for designing Character Cocktails appropriate to the narrative arc—with photos for our website, BnGbooks.com. She's a great mixologist!

A thunderous applause going to the great ladies who edited, edited, and again edited for us. Marty Kutas, Diane Newman, Jan Gohl, and Becky Sloboda, whose attention to detail with their encyclopedic knowledge made this a much better story. Their generous words of praise and kind words of criticism have helped us create the story we hoped to tell.

To each of our friends and allies who have graciously allowed us to use and grow from your experiences, our thanks. You have shown us that it's all about the amazing stories we accumulate through life. You have tolerated and critiqued our thinking out loud as we created this story and studiously ignored our whining through the laborious tasks of editing and rewriting—again, and again, and again. We thank you for whatever reserves you needed to call to the forefront in this process.

We extend our thanks to our friend, Wendy Simms, Pima County, Arizona, Senior Forensic Technician. Our sincere appreciation to this sheriff's organization for allowing us to use Wendy's picture as the prototype of our gal Phoebe Korneal (pronounced Cor-Nell), and using their police vehicle as the backdrop for her photo.

The National Mining and Hall of Fame Museum in Leadville, Colorado, gave us the inspiration for this setting. Their collections highlight the brave women who helped make mining the anchor for the beginnings of Colorado in the 1800s. We live stronger in today's world with this firm understanding of our history as exemplified in museums. Thank you for capturing the reality of the Colorado mining life.

CHARACTER GLOSSARY

Albert Lewis AKA Old Al: Gold Prospector by trade, engineer by the GI Bill, and dead of curious circumstances. He was called Old Al, because he was, well, old and always looked it.

Anne Louise Higgins-Ross: Current matriarch of the Higgins Family and mother of Augusta. She recently moved back to Oresville from Port-en-Bessin, France. After many years she is still not proficient in the art of the French language.

Augusta Higgins Ross-Ledbetter: Owner-Operator of The Last Hurrah copper mine, head of Higgins Family Fortune. She's one of the richest women west of the Mississippi and self-centered enough to maintain the standing.

Bart Masterson AKA Ponytail Guy or Beautiful Man: Police officer in Greenstone, Colorado. Up and coming boyfriend to Phoebe. Rather naive and unskilled when it comes to the opposite sex, but willing to learn.

Bill Diamond: Undersheriff in Green County, major-suck up to Sheriff Joe, step brother to Carrie Jean, and childhood friend to Phoebe back in Salt Lake City.

Billy Baldwin: Owner/operator of the Green County Towing and Recovery Service.

Brian Friedrich: The one and only bartender at the Club, son of the club manager, and steady interest to Carrie Jean.

Carrie Jean O'Brien AKA CJ: Ace (and only) reporter/photographer/and pseudo editor of the daily e-Blast! at the High Country Gazette. She is the childhood friend of Phoebe. Bill Diamond is her step-brother. She is always looking for the next headline.

Chance Watson: Helicopter owner/pilot for Flight for Life. Nephew of Coroner Doc Jon Watson and brother to Laurie Watson, Greenstone Elementary School Principal.

Constance Clark Higgins: Original matriarch of the Higgins Family Oresville fortune in the 1800's, daughter of lucky gold prospectors, Sam and Molly Higgins. Entrepreneur in the start-up days of Colorado, and ruthless businesswoman—deceased.

Doc Jon Watson: Twenty-year coroner in Green County and owner of the only mortuary in Oresville. He is a lover of details, single, and uncle to Laurie Watson and helicopter owner/pilot, Chance.

Ellis Meredith Walker: A bad driver and soon to be ex-wife of Mickey Walker.

Greenstone, Colorado: Located a hundred or so miles east from Oresville and the next-door town to the city of Pikeview.

Hank Williams Klingfus: High school senior and his family's "manager-in-residence" living in Greenstone, Colorado, a hundred miles from Oresville. Past gold prospecting intern/sherpa for Old Al Lewis and pet mule, Rose.

Jesus Garcia: Owner/editor of the local newspaper, High Country Gazette, and high school buddy of Sheriff Joe.

Joe Jackson: Green County Sheriff for way too many years. He was born and raised in Oresville and is now an eternal politician for re-election as sheriff, a family man with four grown daughters, and married to Sweet M&M.

Jorge Tavarez: Retired minister and married to TuTu, chief cook and bottle washer at TuTu's Washateria.

Laurie Watson: Greenstone elementary school principal. A friend of Roz's from Pikeview. Niece of Coroner, Doc Jon Watson and sister of helicopter owner, Chance.

Martha Lewis AKA Queennie: Wife of Old Al Lewis and radiator shop owner in Pikeview, Colorado.

Mary Margaret Jackson AKA Sweet M&M: Married to Sheriff Joe Jackson, school teacher, and native of Oresville.

Michael "Mickey" Walker: New custodian of the Green County office building and soon to be the ex-husband of Ellis Meredith.

Phoebe Korneal: Green County Deputy and detective as needed. Imported from Salt Lake City, she joined her best friends, Bill Diamond and CJ.

Pikeview, Colorado: Big city next door to the small town of Greenstone. Located one hundred or so miles east from Oresville, Colorado.

Rebecca Riney: Native of Oresville and owner of the Buns Up aka the Buns coffee shop and bakery.

Rosalind Marie Beaudreax AKA Roz: Dispatcher at the Sheriff's office. Imported from the bayous of Louisiana and a Cajun beauty.

Rose, the Mule: Longtime pet and companion to deceased Old Al Lewis. Currently living in the front yard at the Higgins mansion.

Rose Mary Thomas: Thirty-year partner to Willie Friedrich and runs the kitchen staff at the B.P.O.E. AKA the Club.

TuTu AKA Gabriella Trujillo Tavarez: Minister, counselor, owner of TuTu's Washateria in Oresville, and philanthropist extraordinaire. Married to Jorge.

Uncle Quinton Garrett AKA Uncle Q: Retired Arkansas Valley assayer and longtime partner to Anne Louise Ross, Augusta's mother.

Willie Friedrich: Perpetual manager and past Exalted Ruler of the B.P.O.E., the Club. Father to Brian, Jennifer and Anne, occasional barmaids at the Club with Brian the consistent and only bartender.

READING GROUP

1. Domestic abuse takes many forms. How has this affected the life and marriage of Mickey and Ellis? How prevalent is domestic abuse in our society? Do you see a prejudice regarding men who are being abused vs women?

2. What do you think are the challenges for women in law enforcement today? In the story, Phoebe moves from a big city in another state to a small mountain town in order to further her career. Can we speculate about the personal opportunities in a small town vs. a big city, especially in law enforcement? What is the trade-offs pros and cons?

3. How do women relate to Augusta in her non-traditional role as owner of a working mine, her lifestyle, and her change of heart at the end of the story? What are the differences between women in nontraditional work in Corporate America vs. small town settings? Can we call out the examples as proof one way or the other—easier or not?

4. How do women relate to Queennie and her unique role in life? Queennie never divorced Old Al. She owns and works in a radiator shop thanks to the funding from Al's gold prospecting. She rides a Harley for pleasure. Do these choices influence how others see her? What are your first thoughts regarding this character?

5. There are several unique women in this story. How do they support each other? What are their differences? Can you give examples of how they support one another? What would you expect to see with this group—small community, high altitude, and newcomers about the same age?

6. What do you think will happen with Phoebe and Beautiful Man? Will their relationship grow? What will make this relationship a challenge to develop? What examples could make it easier? Will distance help or hinder?

7. How is the Elks Club important to the culture of Oresville? What are examples from the story of how the Club "works" for Oresville?

8. Augusta's family history is steeped in the tradition of mining. Why do you think Augusta has chosen the life of a miner rather than the civilized life of a wealthy woman? In the story, what are the examples of her choices? What or who is influencing the changes for Augusta by the end of the story?

There are several characters in this fiction work. Who would you like to see more of in the next book? Please let us know at phoebekorneal@gmail.com. We would love to hear from you! We appreciate your opinions and are happy to answer your questions and your pleas for more!

Books by

GaGa Gabardi and Judilee Butler

A PHOEBE KORNEAL MYSTERY SERIES

BOOK 3

COMING

SOON!

ABOUT THE AUTHORS

Judilee and GaGa at the Sloboda Summer Literary Salon

We stumbled into our collaboration beginning with a short story in the *Mysteries from the Museum* for a fund-raising project for the National Mining Hall of Fame and Museum in Leadville, Colorado. We enjoy using Colorado history for background and the research for these tidbits is both entertaining and rewarding. From this first short story, we were thinking, *Why not take the next step and develop characters, storyline, and a setting all within the context of our joint sense of humor?*

Learning to use technology to jump the hurdles of our distant locations—2,000 miles between our homes—we were able to collaborate, allowing us to develop our character, Phoebe Korneal (pronounced Cor-Nell) and grow a framework around a small mountain town. Each book in our trilogy will touch on a social issue. We are hoping to provide some food for thought and discussion.

The Last Slide is intended to be a fun read. Sit back, enjoy the story and at the end, want to read our next adventure, Book 3 in the Phoebe Korneal Mystery Trilogy! Meantime, we invite you to share questions, comments, and extraneous outbursts at our website BnGbooks.com and by email at PhoebeKorneal@gmail.com.

How can you help us? We want to continue to expand on the world of women in law enforcement today and also the special culture in small communities throughout America.

Share your experiences with us! Even the tiniest of tales rolls into the next chuckle, the unexpected guffaw, or the next wonky tale. It's the stories you share that encourage us to pursue the platform of Phoebe and friends, the Sheriff Department of Oresville, and communities in every state in this great country of America.

Please tell your friends, family and the world about this book. Write a review about *The Last Slide, A Phoebe Korneal Mystery* on Amazon.com. Don't forget our first book, *The Last Hurrah, A Phoebe Korneal Mystery*, that set up the story for this second book. We also thank the judges of the Colorado Authors League for the Finalist Award for Book 1 and also the Bronze Award from the Colorado Independent Publishers Association.

Visit us on our website at BnGbooks.com and share your feedback at PhoebeKoeneal@gmail.com. We are always looking for the next storyline, the next character cocktail, and the next laugh.

⌃⌃⌃

GAGA GABARDI

Graduating from college, my one thought was to leave Minnesota and live where the weather is phenomenal, but I never made it to southern California!

I retired from a career in telecom with a Master's in Project Management, another in Business, and an Advanced Project Degree from Stanford (thank you, corporate world). Completing my private pilot license, I needed money for 'av' fuel . . . back to work—this time consulting, teaching, course development, a welcome change alongside the birth of my first grandson who named me GaGa. Thank you, B.

Writing with Judilee is a way I can add levity within the confines of the pandemic, reach out to others to share our mutual experiences, and fine-tune my storytelling.

Hubby and I live in the Colorado mountain areas. It's an easy pace for us with enough space to enjoy camping, fishing, and riding the rough mountain trails. I can't make up these experiences!

I hope you enjoy *The Last Slide,* get a chuckle here and there, learn a bit regarding Colorado history, and at the end, wonder what happens next.

⋏⋏

JUDILEE BUTLER

Born and raised in New York, I attended the State University of New York at Brockport. After teaching Kindergarten for several years, it was time to leave the cold and snowy winters of upstate New York. Once settled in North Carolina, I completed a Master's Degree in Special Education. While in college, I was hired by IBM and I began a very exciting marketing career in the tech world. That was quite the culture shock.

Twenty years later, with the family safely launched into life, my husband and I retired to the coast of Maine. Three years later the call of trout fishing in the Rockies became too strong for my husband to resist. We happily moved to the beautiful Arkansas Valley in the central mountains of Colorado. Sixteen years later, as life at eight thousand feet took its toll, we decided to move further north into Wyoming, still enjoying the history and beauty of the American West. We take a yearly winter trek to Florida with occasional visits to Port-en-Bessin, France. Maybe I will learn more than three French words in this lifetime.

ABOUT THE AUTHORS

Writing with GaGa has opened up new vistas for me. When most women our age are settling in for a serene period in their lives, we have jumped into the exciting world of writing and promoting our works. Every day is a new challenge. And we wouldn't have it any other way.

We love writing our books and hope you enjoy reading our stories.

GAGA AND JUDILEE are available for discussions, lectures, and select readings: In person, via radio, Zoom, or television. We travel readily over the internet! To inquire about a possible visit, interview, or literary salon, please contact: phoebekorneal@gmail.com

They favor locations such as Colorado, Florida, Wyoming, Minnesota, North Carolina, Arizona and Hong Kong. Inquire soon; scheduling time is of the essence.

phoebekorneal@gmail.com

BnGBooks.com